Toyah Antoinette Snow is the author of *The Ultimate Being* and mother of one daughter. Toyah has dyslexia and has struggled all her life with spelling and reading. She was not able to read until the age of twelve, but once she could, she never stopped. Toyah would read books every opportunity she had, and the love to read inspired her to write. She was once told by a friend, whom she met on her travels around the globe, "You should do what you love and turn that passion into a career." That is when Toyah felt compelled to begin her first novel and venture herself into the world of writing.

I dedicate this book to my beloved daughter, Thea; without you, I wouldn't have found the motivation to finish this book. You brought the light into my once darkened world.

Toyah Antoinette Snow

THE ULTIMATE BEING

AUSTIN MACAULEY PUBLISHERS™

LONDON • CAMBRIDGE • NEW YORK • SHARJAH

A CIP catalogue record for this title is available from the British Library.

ISBN 9781528991551 (Paperback)
ISBN 9781528991568 (ePub e-book)

www.austinmacauley.com

First Published (2021)
Austin Macauley Publishers Ltd
25 Canada Square
Canary Wharf
London
E14 5LQ

Firstly, I would like to acknowledge my mother, Tania O'Driscoll; without your love, support, and help, this would have never been possible.

Also, to my lifelong friend, Shannon Dunphy; to you, I owe the beginning of the foundations this book was created upon. Had you not encouraged me to travel, I may have never written this book. I would also like to thank my sisters, Ciara and Jordan, for all their patience with me during this journey. All in all, I would like to thank my whole family for being the amazing people you are, and for continuing to inspire me to be the best version of myself.

Thank you, Austin Macauley Publishers, for helping my dream come true.

Chapter 1

Today is the day I move. Today is the day I start my new life, new school and new friends. Well, here's to hoping. What if no one wants to be my friend? What if no one likes me? How am I meant to start all over again…?

Those I hold dearest to me. The ones I love have been cruelly ripped away from me.

I have lost everything. As I look back over the recent past events, my heart comes to a complete abrupt halt inside my chest, with a pain so severe, it is like nothing I have ever felt before. Well, that's what it felt like the first time it happened. But now every time I think of them, this happens. I cannot remember a time before this, it feels like it is a part of me now. The pain has become one with me. But I welcome it. Because it means they lived, that I once was able to hold onto them, to hug them. To simply talk to them. But now they are gone. I am all alone in this big scary world. Just waiting and hoping my little sister pulls through and makes it. Then maybe I will not feel as alone, we can help each other through this pain, sharing the weight of the grief we would both hold for our parents. I would no longer keep it all upon my fragile shoulders that were not made to carry the full weight of the loss of my parents at such a brittle young age.

How am I meant to tell her?

'Oh, and by the way, while you were fighting for your life and lying in a hospital bed, I had to bury our parents in the ground. I had to greet all our family, whom I had never met before, and slap on a smile and pretend that I was holding it all together. I had to do it for them. To hold onto the memory of the life that they had lived.'

I relax back in my seat, trying to hold back the tears fighting to get out. How can I still have tears? Inevitably, they will run out. An image of my beautiful mother runs through my mind. Her red hair dancing in the sunlight, as we sit on a sandy beach. Both watching Rose playing in the sand with my father, her husband. The joy on her face, so bright, as the day before us. How can a moment once so perfect now hold so much pain. The last time we would spend as a family. How could any of us have known? My father playing along with Rose, building a sandcastle. He was always so happy to join in and play. Both my mother and father were very attractive people, I had always known they were beautiful. But I had not realised the full extent of their beauty till their death.

You cannot fully know what you have until it is taken away from you. The love they had for Rose and me. The love I had for them. So pure and endless. Oh, what I would give for just one more moment with them.

Why did I survive? It is not fair, why did they have to die, and I live on? Their lives so clearly meant so much more than my own. What am I meant to do with the life I was spared over my parents? What if even my dear sister Rose does not pull through and make it out alive? Why me and not her? The tears are streaming now. Like someone had turned on a tap and left it endlessly running.

Not only have I lost my parents but I have also lost the life I once had. The life I loved. The one I should have never taken for granted. Now I have to leave it all behind. Move not only to a new home but an entirely new country. With new people, new places to learn and a whole new home, where I know no one.

Once I was told I had to pack up and move overseas to a country I had never even been to before, I instantly googled it to get a better idea of where I was going. It is a breath-taking place. A place that could not possibly be real, with its raw beauty. The picture-perfect landscape. It is a place where fairy tales come alive. New Zealand, Aotearoa, the land of the long white cloud.

I landed a good three hours ago now. The plane journey was excruciating. The first flight lasted a whole nine hours, and I thought that was bad until I had to endure the second half, which were a horrendous fourteen hours. When the plane finally landed at its destination, I could not be happier to finally be on land, with my feet firmly planted on the earth beneath me. A shiver runs up my spine with just the thought of the bumpy ride. Air pockets in the sky apparently do not sound like much, but when you are thousands of miles up in the pale blue sky, amongst the fluffy white cotton candy clouds, these very air pockets make your skeleton jump from your very skin.

Now I am sat in the back of a cab, comforted by the earthy smells that swirl through the slightly opened window to the cab door next to me. The light breeze adds to the soothing atmosphere. I am on the way to my new boarding school, staring out at the remarkable picturesque surroundings around me. How can one place hold so much beauty? Mum and dad would love this place. I stop short, remembering the reason I'm adventuring here in the first place. I stop and correct myself. They would have loved it.

Still, till this day, investigations are in motion to figure out what caused the fire in my family home. The one that ended my parent's life. The one that has left my sister fighting for her life in a hospital bed, back in England.

I can still smell the smoke, feel the heat of the autumn toned fiery flames against my skin. The smell of burnt flesh is still lingering. Will it ever go? Will the painful flashbacks ever stop? My arms still smell like burnt smoky hair, the palms of my hands still wrapped in bandages, blistered and roasted from the incandescent heat – yet to fully heal. I tried so hard to free my parents from the burning house, they told me to save Rose first. I promised I would be back for them. I told them to hold on. That everything would be OK. I got her out. I did what they had wanted me to do, and I began to run back to the house to free my parents from being trapped in a room. I had previously tried to pull at the handle but let out a scream when the skin of my hands fused to the blazing metal handle of the door. That was when my parents had told me to run and help Rose before it was too late for all of us.

I was so close. But not close enough. The house exploded into a million pieces, with my parents still embraced in each other's arms stuck for eternity. Now gone. The blast took them away from me. I fell to the ground screaming, screaming for the parents that I had just lost. Not realising the full extent of the very meaning of being gone. Gone forever, and never coming back. I still cannot grasp the concept of never being able to see them again, to see them smile. To laugh.

How can someone exist one moment then not at all the next? How am I ever going to learn to live without them? How am I to ever be happy again? Life is so fragile. So easy to break. It takes but your last breath to end it all. For what was once life is now death. What was once death is now forever. Not knowing the full meaning of the word was bliss but now I wish I could unknow what I now know. For what was once ignorance is now my living nightmare. Gone but never forgotten.

Chapter 2

My cab pulls up in front of my new school. The buildings are enormous, hidden away in the mountains and forest. The greenery is overgrown and cloaking itself all over the walls. If I had not known better, I would think this school was trying to hide. To blend into its natural habitat, the beauty has me standing with my mouth wide open. So shocked. How can this be a school? I hear a bell ring in the distance and it snaps me back to reality. Students start to pile out of the building and head to the field in a stampede, all pushing and shoving past each other, ready to feast, to saturate their hunger. Hurrying to freedom. It must be lunchtime…

A few students stare over to me, curious to see me standing there with all my suitcases, wide-eyed and in awe of my surroundings. Could I really make myself any more obvious as to who I am, the new girl, the newly orphaned and the outcast, who now has to find her way into an already made friend group? The school year has already started, I'm joining halfway through term two.

Could it get any worse? Am I going to be that lonely girl sitting by herself at the lunch table? With not a friend in sight. Have I not been through enough already that now I have to endure the uproar of teenagers, the awkwardness of going through puberty and thinking we all know what life is about when we know far from it. Acting out what we believe portrays being an adult. What do we really know but nothing? We are yet to unfold the secrets of life itself. Instead of helping each other, we separate into small groups we like to call 'cliques' and pull each other down, when we need to be lifted the most!

My train of thought is interrupted by a deliberate cough, to try to gain my otherwise indulgent attention. Why, I will never understand. I blink repeatedly. Trying to make sense of what I see. Those children that had moments before been walking by, gawking at me as if I was from Mars, are now standing right in front of me trying to get my attention. *What do they want? Are they here to just patronise me?*

One of the guys was tall and handsome, with chiselled features like nothing I had ever seen before, as if angels themselves had taken it upon themselves to create perfection. His eyes bore down on to me. The striking blue, piercing through my ability to speak. *What is this? Why am I feeling so lost and insignificant?* Then all of a sudden, my emotions flip, to feeling happiness like I had never felt before. *I feel so lifted I could practically walk on clouds. What is happening? I have no reason to feel this way.* I pull myself out of it and shake off the foreign feeling.

My mouth hanging wide open, catching flies without my knowing, shocked by my very own emotions. I genuinely am losing it.

The tall, handsome boy stood in front of me takes a hasty step back and turns himself towards his friends without ever turning his back to me.

"Look at her, she has not got a clue at all. The look on her face. She is petrified. She doesn't know why she is here."

The girl to his right steps forward, her long jet-black hair falls around her like a cloak. Her eyes as dark as pools of tar.

"How is that even possible, she must know where she is. Or does she not belong here. Is she lost?" the raven-haired girl snarls her comment nastily directing it towards me without even trying to hide it.

The tall, handsome one looks back to me now, with a knowing look on his face. He places a hand on my shoulder and replies with a cheeky smile,

"No, she is not lost, she belongs here."

Raven hair turns to him with shock evidently present in her eyes.

"How could you possibly know that? You have yet to even say hello to the poor girl," her tone becoming angrier at the evident disgust of the situation at hand.

"Because I just messed with her emotions trying to see what she would do, what power she holds. She might not know what she is but she is powerful. No one has ever been able to push me out of their heads before. Let alone stop it in its track. Without me being the one to stop it," the beautiful one's words are oozing with pride.

I do not understand why they are. It feels wrongly placed. Like it does not belong being attached to the words flowing from his blood-red lips.

Confused, I step back from his grasp. *What are they talking about? Have I really been shipped to a mental hospital? Has everyone lost hope for me?*

"I'm sorry, how rude of me. My name is Romeo. And yours is?"

Finally, I can put a name to the tall, handsome one; Romeo. I let his name swirl around inside my head, soaking it up. I mumble like an idiot.

"Romeo?"

"Yes, that is what I said. Are you OK?" His brows fold into themselves, unsure of my reaction.

I stumble back, sickened by my behaviour.

"Oh sorry, it has been a long journey here, I'm afraid I'm not quite with it."

I try to salvage what I have left of my dignity but then I'm rudely interrupted by the raven-haired girl.

"Not yourself? Not there at all if you ask me." Again, her words are surrounded by double meaning.

Romeo cuts back at her, stopping her in her tracks.

"Sylvia, stop it, this is not the time for one of your annoying temper outbursts."

Romeo turns back to me.

"Sorry about her, she is all bark and no bite," Romeo looks back and forth between Sylvia and me.

Sylvia, in return, gives him an evil stare.

"So, do you have a name? Or shall I make one up for you?" Her eyes now shooting daggers towards me. If looks could kill, I would be dead before I have even had the chance to walk through the school corridors.

Shit, I must look like a complete tool. I hurry to reply, not wanting to prolong my lunacy.

"No, my name is Victoria, you can call me Tori for short. I have just arrived here in New Zealand."

I take a quick glance behind me to see the cab driver has already left and had removed the rest of my belongings, leaving them behind me in the car park. *Great! I truly am stuck here now.* I take a deep breath in, to steady my frantic nerves. *Breathe, Victoria, everything will be OK. What is the worst that can happen?*

"Do you need a hand with carrying all your bags up to your dorm room. I can help if you would like? Show you around. You know, to be your trusted tour guide?"

I cannot help myself but return a sheepish grin. I stare into his eyes just wishing I could look into them forever.

"So, I take that as a yes."

Romeo takes it upon himself to be my tour guide for the school and starts heading towards my bags. Just before grabbing the two big suitcases, he looks up to me then. Smiling with his crystal-clear eyes, his eyes ask the question before he can.

"Yes, I would never refuse your help," I flirt terribly as he laughs at my apparent lack of skills.

With that, he picks up my suitcases as if they are as light as a feather. Not faltering once. I know for a fact they are so much heavy, I had to pay extra for them being over the maximum requirement.

I quickly scoop up my duffle bag along with my handbag and laptop. I follow behind the handcrafted masterpiece that happens to be willingly helping me to my room.

"Romeo, don't forget to tell the new girl to stop by the office to pick up her books and class schedule," Sylvia shouts over her shoulder to remind Romeo sarcastically, her words oozing with the hidden meaning behind *'The New Girl!'* comment.

The others who had been stood with him stare after us. Two of the guys had not said a word, not even to introduce themselves, but were now chatting away to Sylvia and another girl who I had not yet got the name of.

She was beautiful, she stood tall in comparison to Sylvia but by no means to the two guys. Her hair cut in a stylish long bob, with a mixture of browns and urban tones naturally placed, perfectly executed by her stylist. The two guys also appeared to be very handsome. One with white blond hair tied back into a man bun, placed on top of his head. The other with shabby brown hair, short on the sides with wavy strands flowing down into his eyes.

I take one last look at them before catching up with Romeo I hear my name travel through the wind as it passes through their lips. Great! I'm here five minutes, and I'm already being talked about. Whatever happened to keep a low profile? Romeo slows down so he can be in stride with me. Clearing his throat abruptly before engaging conversation with me.

"So, what brings you to the other side of the world? I'm guessing you have come here from England by the sound of your posh British accent."

Great! He thinks I'm a posh twat from England. I reply to him, while trying to tone down my accent if that is possible, "Yes, I am from England. Thought I would come here and check out the scenery. You know to change things up a bit."

He looks at me then. With a look that tells me he knows I'm hiding the real reason I have come here. But he chooses to not push it any further. For that, I am grateful and find myself falling for him that little bit more. I do not know how I would be able to tell anyone the series of tragic events leading up to me having to travel thousands of miles, from my hometown to somewhere I have never been to before. They would think I am a lost cause, a charity case. I wince at the thought. I decided then and there that I will not tell anyone about my past.

I slow my pace down, as I think back to our encounter, thinking what did he mean I do not know who I am. Of course, I do. I take a deep breath and pluck up the courage to ask.

"Romeo, what did you mean by I do not know who I am?"

He stops then, turning to look directly at me, with a slight smile turned up at one side. He replies with an uneasiness, not being sure how to approach.

"I do not think I am properly equipped with explaining it to you correctly, and for that, I am sorry. But if you would like, I could take you somewhere after I help with your bags, to help answer your queries?"

I look up at him with a delicate smile, I do love the way he speaks. He sounds so confident. Almost like from another era. Could he be any more perfect?

"Yes, I would love that, only if it is not too much to ask. I do not want to be a burden to you."

I take my phone from my pocket, checking to see what the time is; my phone has automatically changed to the correct time zone without me having to do it.

He starts walking again then, laughing as he goes.

"You a burden? Do not be absurd, it would be a privilege but do not thank me yet. You may not like what you hear or see."

I follow after him, like a love-struck child thinking this over. May not like what I see? How bad could it be? We walk in silence as we round the next corner, then head up three flights of stairs. I stop three or four times to catch my breath and readjust my hold on my belongings. Once we finally reach the third floor, I take in a deep breath, before complaining about the lack of lifts at this school.

"Have you guys ever heard of lifts before, you know those things that go up and down, and help with carrying heavy loads. Instead of having to transport them up three flights of stairs. And please tell me for the sake of all that is holy, this is the floor I am staying on?"

Romeo turns around with an amused expression on his face, with a hint of mischief in his eyes.

"Lifts? I have never heard of such a thing, I am afraid we still have five more floors to go up. You will be OK, won't you, my queen?"

Queen? Who does he think he is calling queen? I, for sure, hope it is not me.

Is he really trying to attempt my accent too? It's pretty good, not going to lie. But I am not going to tell him that and give him the satisfaction. If I dare tell him, I am sure his head will explode from the compliment. One thing is for sure, he does not need the boost of confidence. His presence is already drowning in him being full of himself but yet it is not too much. He seems to have the right balance, which is why I do not want to tip the scales for him.

"Five more flights of stairs? You have to be kidding me?" I expel in exasperation.

Romeo bursts into laughter and doubles over forward.

"What is so funny?"

Romeo puts his hand up then and indicates with one index finger to give him a minute. I huff in annoyance and wait for him to come back to his senses. He stands up, with the biggest grin on his face. Like he just won a Nobel prize.

"Your face was priceless when I told you we had five more to go." He laughs some more before continuing.

"You should have seen it. I have never seen someone so shocked but pissed off about having to walk upstairs, oh and by the way, we do know what a lift is, and we also have a lift. I just thought after your long flight, you might appreciate the exercise; you know to get the blood pumping."

He stops to laugh again, at my reaction of finding out there is a lift, and I just hurled my way up those stairs for no reason other than his amusement. *Great.* I storm off down the hall, just wanting to get to my room to hide away from all this craziness.

"Tori?"

I spin around on my heels, annoyed at being stopped.

"What?" I scold.

"You are going the wrong way; it's this way. Unless you want to sleep in the boys' dorm."

I turn around and head back the other way.

"I knew that, how do you know where my room is in the first place?" I shrug off the embarrassment and try to play it cool, knowing full well that Romeo would not buy it. But I try anyway.

He stops laughing and teasing then.

"You knew where you were going?" Romeo goes to make a remark about the comment I had just made but decides to let it slide, for now anyway. He stares at me, this time with a sly one-sided smile trying to escape from its confinement.

"If I had known you already knew your way around, I would not have accepted their offer."

The look in his eyes tells me he has left the bait for me to decide what to do with it, either find out what he means or never know. Should I take the bait and play along or pretend I could not care less. In theory, I do care, so I decide to amuse the idea.

"Whose offer? Accept what?"

I curl my fingers into the palms of my hands, my nails almost breaking the skin from the ever-growing frustration of the situation.

"I was told you were to arrive today and to show you to your room."

Great! Here's me thinking he is doing this out of the kindness of his heart. But in reality, he has been assigned to. I just keep on feeling better, with yet another hit to my ego. Maybe I am the one who is big-headed after all, thinking he would just offer to help me out of the blue. Who do I think I am? The queen?

He stops in front of an old oak door about seven feet tall, with detail so delicate and extravagant, I reach out to touch it and trace the design. Romeo watches me with interest.

"That is our native Maori tribal design that has been hand-carved."

I stare at it in amazement.

"Wow, it is beautiful." My fingers continue to trail along the grooves in the crafted wood.

Romeo stares down at me then and takes a deep breath, whispering under his breath.

"Not as beautiful as you are."

I look up at him, confused.

"Sorry, what did you say?" I reply without ever breaking my interest from the workmanship in front of me.

"Nothing, just that this is your room, you have one other roommate and that I will be back up in half an hour to get you, to take you to get your answers if you would still like?"

I reply with an assertive nod of the head.

"Yes, please, that would be great, and thank you for your help."

"OK, I will leave you to get settled and unpacked. If you need anything, I'm on the fifth floor. But I will see you soon. Bye."

With that, I watch as Romeo turns around and starts making his way down the hall. I stare after him until I can no longer see him, with only his silhouette to show that he has continued down the corridor. I watch it dancing freely along the walls in the fading sunlight, shining through the floor to ceiling windows on the outermost part of the building.

I then face my door, ready to meet my new roommate. The atmosphere around me feels still and quiet, so quiet the hair on my arms stand up on edge, my nerves getting the better of me. *OK, I can do this, she is probably one of the nicest girls I could room with unless with my unfortunate luck I could end up roomed with Sylvia for the whole school year. Now wouldn't that be exciting?* I sigh in exasperation; I am just being silly and hypersensitive to my new surroundings, which is to be expected.

As I reach down to unlock the door after knocking three times, I decide to open it myself, maybe she has her headphones in, perhaps she might just be asleep, who knows? I push the door open then. Well, I more fall into it while I still try and fumble around with my bags, I trip over one of the straps to my duffle bag that had managed to escape the grasp of my hand. Sending me flying, profoundly flat onto my still bandaged hands and knees, pushing back the neatly placed bandages that had been protecting my healing hands, knocking one of my bags into the chest of drawers nearest to the door. I look up to see the full extent of the damage I had caused in the literal seconds of being her new roommate. I bet she will take one look at me and tell me to leave, running to the first teacher she sees asking if they can have me reassigned to another room!

But once I do look up and take a second to look around the room, I notice the room is empty with no person in sight. Well, I guess that could have been one of the other reasons she had not opened the door for me; she is not even present to do so; why I didn't think of that? I will never know.

Oh well, I am incredibly thankful that she is not here; otherwise, this could have gone a whole other way; looks like my clumsy antics will go unnoticed this time.

I roll over onto my back, looking up at the ceiling. I take a deep breath in, as I take in the intricate detail that trails along with the ceiling. It looks magnificent, the carving and woodwork from the door seem to have been incorporated into the main room, leading the design up along the ceiling. The carvings telling a story of their own, I must look more into the native Maori history so I can learn what it is this masterpiece of craftsmanship means. The story that has been laid out before me, waiting to be understood.

I lift my right palm up to my face, taking in the slight carpet burn that I had inflicted onto my not yet fully healed flesh, only prolonging my hands' recovery process from my burnt palm, on the trip into my new room. I joke around inside my head, *Did you have a nice trip, Tori? Oh yes, I sure did, got the postcard and sent it your way.*

I laugh at myself. *Oh, I am insanely funny,* I make a sarcastic remark towards myself. With that I turn over into a downward dog and walk my hands, up ignoring the constant thumping from my resistant palms, begging me to be kind to them, I continue till I am leaning upright with my hands placed at my feet.

I stay there for a little longer, letting the stretch work its magic, I should do some yoga later. It will help get my blood flowing around my body and legs, to help prevent any blood clots forming from the long flight here. I slowly make my way up, pressing my hands into each other, bringing them into my chest and taking a steady breath in and out through my nose.

I open my eyes to finally take in my new surroundings. I suppose this is going to be my new home for the next few years, three if I'm lucky. Who knows I might get high enough grades to stay till year thirteen. What's it called here? The seventh form, is it? I really need to get a handle on this new terminology for this school and well, the country. It's crazy to think that the whole world operates in such drastically different ways to one another. It does keep to the appeal of travel, otherwise I suppose if every country were the same, there would be no need for travel at all, you would not need to go outside the comfort of your own life, to see how everyone else lives their lives, as it would be equal to your very own. Oh how boring life would be then? We should all be grateful for all the unique differences that make us, us. For if it weren't for these personal differences, we would all be scarily alike.

With that thought I move into the en suite. I make a note of the bay window facing out onto the school grounds. I will have to find a good book and spend some time placed inside the window with a cup of coffee. I reminisce by remembering the pleasure I experienced from the bay window I had at home in the upstairs hallway, the possibilities and promise of relaxation and the time I can see myself spending cooped up there.

I continue on my way to the en suite, which opens up through two full-length mirrored doors. As I go to pull them open, I take a look at my appearance, taking in the dark imprinted sunken circles around my eyes that seem to be a permanent addition to my once bright and hopeful facial structure, the last few months have really taken a toll on my general health as well as my physical appearance. I look at where there used to be toned definition of muscle from all the sports I took part in, now I can see my skeleton, trying to break free of my now paled sun-kissed skin, malnourished from my lack of appetite due to falling into an unavoidable depression.

Like the person, who is still inside me somewhere, is trying to break free, from the shell of what is left of the happy go-free girl I once was. Not too long ago either, but you will be amazed how one life-altering experience can completely change you as an individual.

I look at the person who stands before me with her long cascading hair, falling in limp waves around my middle section and shoulders. They no longer hold the life they once had either; once a shiny, healthy mousey brown. With naturally bleach blonde highlights playing its way through the volumized waves, now sit dull and lifeless; like the person I now see before me, trying to escape the lifeless shell of the body I am stuck in, being here might do me some good, fresh start and all.

The only thing that has brightened since that awful night is my eyes, and that's only because my hair, which was once full of bounce and colour, are now darkened along with the shadowed rings around my eyes, which has undoubtedly led to my eye colour now intensifying?

Bright silver with playful sparks of blue shooting through, the odd specks of green and purple, my eyes have always played a role of pulling a person's attention towards my face; to say they are unique is an understatement. Some people sit there in wonder over them, saying how if they could, they would wish to have eyes that looked like mine.

Others making nasty comments saying they make me look like a freak, my mum always told me they were the ones who were most jealous of them. People can indeed be so mean, even to someone as young as I had been, when I was first told that my eyes did not look right that I should be ashamed of them. I was only four years old when my mum's workmate came by to pick up some documentation for a case they were currently working on. To say my mum was not happy is precisely right, she told her to stick it where the sun don't shine, and to never set foot in her home again.

We went out for ice cream after that, walking along the Brighton pier. She told me I should never let anyone like her workmate dampen the light that shines from within me. That I was lucky enough to have that pure light shine from the inside, out through my eyes, that I was to do amazing things in my lifetime and to always tread lightly when it came to choosing what path of light I would want to walk. To never let anyone tell me what I should do, to always listen to what's inside of me to lead me in the right direction to get what I deserve and most desire from my life.

I guess that was her way of trying to prepare me for life without her. I do not think either of us was aware how soon it would be that I would be walking this earth alone.

I turn the right tap on in the bathroom and splash my face with some cold water. I look back to my bags, thinking of having to unpack now was a task I did not want to do. So instead, I go back to my bags and grab out some new clothes to change into.

I ruffle through my stuff to find my toiletries, so I can hop into the shower and fully freshen up, hopefully that might bring back the slightest bit of light that I have lost, to feel like me again. I chuck my towel over my shoulder, closing the bathroom doors behind me. I turn on the shower, deciding that would be best, as Romeo would be back soon to get me.

I turn the heat up, wanting it to soak into my aching muscles. I will have a bath sometime during the week, once I have settled in and have more time.

Chapter 3

I walk beside Romeo, as we approach what seems to be a metal structured stadium. We make our way up to the middle bench, as we walk single file down to the end of the seat row. I would not usually willingly sit this close but as I am with Romeo and he is the one showing me where to go, I sit with him. I would typically prefer to sit as far back as possible out of the way of all the other students. Let's be honest, I would sit as far away from just general people altogether.

After a while of sitting and listening to the endless chatter around me, slowly getting louder and louder as more students pile into the stadium.

Romeo's friends from earlier shout out to him, eagerly wanting to gain his attention, he signals for them to come over and join us. I ask Romeo what the other girl's name is, as she waves up to me. Confused, I look behind me, to see if she is waving to someone else. But she is not.

Romeo then replies.

"That is Willow, she is very excited to meet you, and to get to know you. You are the famous Miss Victoria Luna-Maddicks, after all."

Shocked by the statement he had just made, I shoot back a hurried reply, confused.

"Famous? What are you smoking at this school? I am not famous, far from it. Sorry to disappoint."

Willow reaches us then, followed by the rest of the gang. She joins in on the conversation, mentioning what has been said.

"Once word got out, about who arrived at our gates this morning, rumours of who you are have spread around like wildfire. Is it true you survived a building catching on fire, then exploding?"

Her words soaked in her strong, laid back accent, making me have to listen more studiously.

I sit up straighter then, caught off guard. How could anyone possibly know this? My heart starts pounding in my chest. Tears welling up involuntary. I go to get up and run as far away as I can. But Romeo stops me, by placing his hand on my shaking knee, whispering into my ear.

"It will be all OK, I got you."

And with that, a rush of warmth and ease washes over me. Stopping my panic attack in its tracks. I welcome the feeling as it continues to flow over me.

I still do not understand how he can have this effect on me. Do I love him? I shake that ridiculous thought from my mind. I barely know him; how could I possibly be in love with someone I do not know. There must be another way to explain the effect he has over me.

Right now, I am not complaining and am undeniably content with not knowing as it is like my own personal walking therapist; one touch and I appear to be momentarily cured of the turmoil inside my mind. I guess, I will need to continue seeing him for follow-ups, to have a sustained effect on my current mental well-being. Of course, I cannot get enough already, a welcomed feeling I have grown to adore in such a short time. I have never had the instant pleasure of feeling this emotional release, especially quite like this feeling before. It is a nice change from constantly feeling on edge.

I am taken aback by my sudden confidence to confront Willow; she may not realise the full extent of what she said would have affected me so. But that is why I must tell her. I made a promise to myself not to speak a word of it to anyone but as it looks like word has gotten out anyway, I might as well put all the rumours to bed. I will just have to tell them the truth, of what really happened that frightful night.

"Willow, is it?" I ask in a harsh tone, regretting it as soon as I say the words aloud, not really wanting to sound so rude and harsh.

Willow looks at me then, her face showing all signs of confusion by my tone of voice, she rushes to reply. Not sure what to expect.

"Yes, that is my name." She stares me down, waiting for me to respond.

"Do you not see it in your best interest to get all your facts straight before blurting out the first thing that comes to your mind; your words could hurt someone."

"I'm so sorry, I didn't mean to offend you. I was simply curious and thought best to ask the source of the rumours to get the real story."

I can see the rich shadow of the spreading pink blush that inches its way to her hairline, as it becomes increasingly evident that dear Willow is ashamed of the ordeal playing out in front of the crowded stadium full of prying ears.

But even with noticing these significant details, I cannot seem to hold back the outburst of anger that has clearly been held in far too long – leaving Willow to get the wrongly directed brunt of it.

"Let's get one thing straight, it is not a story. It is my life you are referring to."

Willow begins to apologise but I stop her before she has a chance by raising my hand up to indicate not to bother to continue. As I do, I look from her to Romeo then to the rest of the gang of friends, before telling them the truth. Am I ready to do this? Can I? Before I allow myself to back out of what I had already started, I begin to tell them what had happened.

"If you really must know what happened, I will tell you." I take a deep breath before going on. Steadying myself for what I have to say.

"I was not inside the blazing building when it exploded, as I was standing outside next to my little sister Rose. I had to get her out of our raging, burning home. I went to go back to help my parents get out but when I turned around to head back, the house vividly exploded right before Rose and I, killing my parents who were trapped inside."

I had not realised I had raised my voice, it sounded angrily sad. Like I was about to break down. I stop to get a hold of the tears threatening to get out once again. I will not allow myself to cry in front of all these strangers. Everyone around me who had been listening grew quiet. Then all of a sudden, a voice over a microphone tells everyone to take their seats at once as the training begins. I have never been so grateful for the attention to be averted away from me. Romeo leans over to me then, speaking so only I can hear him.

"Are you OK? We can leave if you would like?"

"No, it is OK. Thank you. Just give me a minute to collect myself."

Romeo nods his head to indicate he heard me, then faces his attention back to where it is needed.

"Are you ready for what you're about to witness?"

I am momentarily distracted by the thought of what it could possibly be.

I am surprised as to how many students have turned up to the stadium, it must be the whole school here. Perfect! That means everyone would have seen the little scene that had played out before them…

Willow has shuffled her way along the bench to place herself next to me, on the other side from Romeo, she leans over.

"Hey, Victo—I mean Tori. I am sorry about before, I should have kept my mouth shut. You know what students can be like, they love making anything they hear to be dramatised completely out of context, you know? Kind of like Chinese whispers," Willow nervously plays with the cuticles of her nails, waiting for me to accept her apology,

She didn't have to come all the way over here after I just reacted the way I did.

"Thank you, that means a lot for you to apologise, you didn't have to."

Well, she kind of did but so do I. I send a half-hearted smile her way as a peace offering.

"Yes, I did, me and my big mouth gets me in trouble quite a lot. Still, haven't learned to think before I say anything to be fair," Willow laughs at herself, and I join in with her.

After a while, we forget why we are even laughing to begin with. I reach my hand out in an offer of a handshake.

"Friends?" I look to her, waiting for her to extend her own hand.

"Friends," she continues our handshake before laughing hysterically.

"What?" I ask.

"What's up with the handshake? Is it a British thing?" Willow says, unceasingly through her laughter.

With that, I swat her with the back of my hand playfully. I sigh into my seat, with a real smile placed on my face. It has been a while since I have had one of those, maybe this place won't be so bad after all.

Chapter 4

Flash, *Bang!* A car comes flying out of the air from nowhere. Straight into the ground, where someone had been standing just seconds before.

A member of the faculty had come out into the middle of the field like they do in baseball games in America, announcing the teams who would be going against each other in the level two battle. They had continued to lay out the ground rules, telling them what they can and cannot do and to always make sure they're looking out for each other's safety.

"We do not want any first-year student's death on our hands just because you could not follow some simple rules and regulations, do you hear me?!"

The teacher who I had yet to meet, lifts his hands into the air, creating the air around him to shift and shimmer from the grass field that had once been before us, to an obstacle course made for the students to test their abilities.

"What the hell was that? Is that person OK? Why is nobody doing anything to help them?" I look around to see everyone still seated, watching the carnage in front of them. Romeo is the only one to answer me.

"He's fine, he has the ability to heal fast," followed by saying under his breath "the lucky dickhead. I could have done with that when training with Mark."

He shakes his head in annoyance.

I look on, unable to believe what I am seeing. The guy I had just seen squashed by a car, which had just appeared out of thin air, crawls out from beneath the wreckage. How could someone possibly survive that? Before I have the chance to process this, fireballs begin to shoot out of the girl's hand on the field, who appears to be on the boy's side that had miraculously survived being crushed by a flying vehicle. They go off uncontrollably, hitting everywhere but her target in front of her. Romeo makes a comment to his friends.

"She really needs to work on her target practice before she hurts herself or worse, an innocent."

His friends agree with him, before turning back to watch the fight in front of them.

This is training, more like a fight to the death. The opponent, on the other side, calls forward the guy to his right to defend. He starts throwing what looks to be disks of electricity from his hand and using them as a footpath up into the air, leaving him hovering above the other side of teammates. He stops once he has a good position and begins to fire electrical impulses, of wildly spinning energy plates at his opponents.

He does not stop until a fireball hits him and throws him off balance, making him fall off his energy ring and come crashing down onto the field below. Before I can see if he hits the ground or not, a fireball comes racing towards me. Frightened and unable to protect myself, I drop to the ground and under my seat but the fireball never makes it to me, as a blue layer of some sort of shield makes it bounce off and distinguishes it, making it fizzle out to nothing.

I stay where I am for a moment, trying to make sense of what is happening around me. As I do, Romeo, my saviour once again lets out a comforting hand for me to hold onto. I pull myself back up onto my seat, looking around to make sure the surrounding area is safe. A guy from the row behind makes a comment.

"Is it your first time to one of these?"

As I do not reply, he continues,

"You're welcome, by the way."

Romeo steps in then.

"Yes, this is her first time. Do you not know who she is?" before he has a chance to answer he does so for him.

"She is Victoria Luna-Maddicks."

By just hearing my name, the guy sits a little further back than necessary in his seat as he begins to apologise, I look to Romeo then. I am infuriated by him answering for me.

"Who do you think you are? I am more than capable of speaking for myself, I do not need you to fight my battles for me, thank you very much."

The guy behind me, who had just scurried back into his seat, begins to chuckle to himself before Romeo shoots him a warning look for him to stop. With that, I stand up to leave, not wanting to be here for a moment longer. What have I gotten myself into? Better yet, where have my family sent me?

I storm off down the stairs and make my way through a crowd of people huddled around in one of the underpasses that lead to the exit. I bump into one of the girls and apologise quickly. She replies with a swift rude remark.

"Watch where you're going, would you? You wouldn't want to end up like the last person who got in my way."

I hurry on, not bothering to respond, just wanting to find a way out. I need to leave this place as soon as I can. I then break into a sprint all the way back up to my dorm room, not stopping once to catch my breath, or to answer a concerned person asking if I am OK, as I rush past them in a stream of tears. Frightened, and wishing my parents where here to save me from all this craziness. *Am I dreaming?* I really hope I am.

Once I finally reach my dorm room, I unlock it. Entering inside, I go straight to my stuff and start packing it all back up into my bags. Thankfully, I had not managed to fully unpack everything before Romeo had come to collect me, to show me what I had just seen on the school field, wishing I had never gone, now slightly realising why he had told me not to thank him yet. But that was before I had a FIREBALL come hurtling towards my head. I can now not get out of here fast enough. I turn around once I have finished packing all my things. As I go to reach for the door to leave this freak show of a place, a tall, beautiful blonde girl walks through the door, stopping me on my quest of escaping. She looks at me, then to my bags.

"Going somewhere?" she asks in her alluring voice.

"I do not have time to talk, sorry, I need to get out of here now."

I go to push past her but she stops me before I can get out of the door.

"It's Victoria, right?" she looks at me then waiting for a reply but I do not bother, not wanting to waste her time.

"I'm only asking as I do not want to have a strange girl in my dorm room, I am only assuming you are, as you have your bags with you. So, you must not be here to burgle the place, I hope."

I look at her then.

"Yes, I am Victoria but I prefer to be called Tori. Not that it matters as I am leaving."

I struggle to push back a stray hair into place, while still balancing all my belongings, as I edge my way further to freedom.

"Leaving? You only just got here, why on earth would you want to leave this place?" she laughs to herself.

"Why wouldn't anyone? This place is making me go insane, I'm seeing things that cannot possibly be happening, there must be something in the air messing with my mind," I fire back.

She looks at me then, with a look on her face of understanding. Great! She feels sorry for me.

"You do not know why you are here, do you?" she asks the question more to herself than me but continues on as if I had answered anyway.

"Do you know who you are? What you are capable of? Do you even realise what you can do, and how many people wish they were you?"

I look at her stunned. Why does everyone keep saying this to me?

"What do you mean by this? How can I possibly not know who I am? I am me," I shrug in defeat.

"I honestly cannot believe you do not know who you are and what you can do," she gestures around herself, to elaborate on her words further.

"Please tell me, enlighten me. Be the one to shine the light on this shitty day," I reply, frustrated by the whole situation. "Who am I then?"

Chapter 5

After a well-deserved rest, and a gruelling explanation of what this school is supposed to be about from Ellie, Romeo and I decide to take a walk outside along the grounds. I bathe in the outstanding beauty that I see before me and look to Romeo. I ask him,

"Where are we? I had never been to New Zealand before the day I arrived at this school."

I look back through my memories, remembering how completely lost I had felt. I remember trying to look at a map to get my bearings.

Ellie still had not answered all my questions, she had been vague but full of information on the history of the school I now attend. It was enlightening, if that, but still I do not know why I am here myself. Romeo continues to stare intently as I speak.

"I remember reading about a place called Papatoetoe?"

As we continue to walk along, I absent-mindedly play with my hair, pulling it back into a ponytail.

"I had flown into Auckland, the taxi driver drove me all the way here. I had asked him a few times where he was taking me."

I exhale frustratingly, remembering how I had felt.

"I had asked him what part of New Zealand we were going to. I remember driving for about two, three days. It's all kind of a blur."

I stumble slightly as I forget where I'm walking, tree branches appear beneath the earth. I feel their laughter as I look down, remembering to watch where I place my feet. I walk now lifting them higher, picking up my pace, walking with more determination as I get more frustrated looking back at the situation.

Romeo had reached out to catch me, without a second thought, like it was second nature. He moves when I move, our silhouettes entwining as one. He mimics my movements without realising; subconsciously, feeling at ease by my side. Intently listening to my every word while I carry on rambling, with no slight detail going unmissed. I continue…

"We had made a couple of stops on the way to rest and tend to our bodily needs. We drove past a theme park named 'Rainbows End' after we had left the airport. We even went through the 'Bay of Plenty Region'."

I stop suddenly, Romeo continues walking for a few unnoticed moments, not realising that I had stopped. When he does, he turns around to look at me. His face full of emotion, full of questions, unsure whether to ask, so he simply speaks the words.

"Are you OK?"

As he does, he walks back towards me, where I stand frozen.

"Yes, I am fine. We had stopped at a petrol station for snacks and a toilet break, I had brought the map out with me." I look down at my hands remembering holding it in them.

"I had been absentmindedly reading as I walked, I must have left it on the side, in the girls' toilets. Because after that I lost track of where we were heading."

I continue to stand where I had stopped moments before, trying to recall every detail of my journey here.

"We had stopped at Tauranga, is it?"

I let Romeo's hand slide into mine, as he answers to my query.

"Yes, there is a place in the north island called 'Tauranga', it is situated in the 'Bay of Plenty'."

He smiles down to me, with a cheeky twinkle in his eye because right then, he decides to pick me up and throw me over his shoulder, tickling me in my weak spot that he could not possibly know about but Romeo seems to know things that no one should.

Not in a bad way; I feel a connection with Romeo like we have known each other for years, instead of mere days. I feel at ease when I am with him, like his very presence has a calming effect on me. I crave it, I think he does too. Ever since we sat next to each other at dinner last night, in between Ellie and my conversation. He had come over to sit with us and even had some insight about the school, filling in where Ellie could not. It was nice. Of course, I found out that Ellie loves to talk, and she continued to until this morning, even throughout breakfast; that is when Romeo offered me his hand and an escape route. I think he could tell that I had taken in enough information and that if I had to endure any more, I would have simply imploded.

I begin to laugh uncontrollably, trying to gasp for air in between. Romeo takes it upon himself to explain where I was at this very moment, I struggle to hear what he is saying over my own laughter.

"You, my sweet Victoria, are in the 'South Island of New Zealand'. The school you now reside in is situated amongst the mountains which we are located in 'Milford Sound'."

That's when Romeo puts me down and I see it as we draw closer to the clearing. I can see two huge mountains on either side, with water running between them rapidly, I look down to the left, as I hear some voices. Romeo pulls me down out of sight.

"Get down, you cannot let anyone see you up here."

I look to him, confused. He sees the question playing across my galaxy refractured prism-coloured eyes, leaning into my elegant shaped nose that now touches the tip of Romeo's nose. I hadn't realised how close we had become. I look into his endless whirlpool of carefully placed slivers of ocean blue eyes. We get lost momentarily gazing into each other's souls but our trance gets broken by the sound of oncoming voices. Romeo looks back, not wanting the moment to end.

He looks seductively into my eyes, showing me their true depth, the spectrum of the vast shades of blues, dancing together in perfect sync, creating a mix of tones so perfect that they could only belong to him, to go along with the rest of his angelic perfection. Just when I think he is about to lean in and kiss me for the very first time, he turns his head rapidly away, hearing something I had not. He turns back to look at me then, his lips moving. I watch them, not hearing what he had been saying until he has to repeat himself again.

"Hey, you?"

The smile plastered across his features show me how much he is enjoying watching me struggle to keep my hands to myself.

"Can I get your attention back up here, please? We need to get over there and try to navigate these people away from here, we cannot risk them accidentally stumbling into the location of the school, it is cloaked but better to be safe than sorry, right?"

He laughs at my lack of assertiveness, my eyes still watching as his lips move. I look up to him, to see his boyish grin blissfully light up his entire face. He holds back the laugh that he had dared to let out moments before.

"You, Victoria Luna-Maddicks, are unearthly beautiful." With that, I could not control it a moment longer. If he's being a gentleman and letting me make the final decisions, I choose that I want to kiss him right now. I dive into his arms and plant my hungry lips to his. He eases in at first but then his lips match my hunger and we fall to the ground lost in the moment.

As we do, we end up rolling uncontrollably down the uneven, rocky dirt mountain, through its terrain of unmade pathways. Not caring enough to stop ourselves, only coming to a full stop as we smash our entwined bodies straight into a towering tree, cascading its leaves around us and over the carnage we had caused, disrupting the natural order of the forest that has grown freely and untouched for many, many years.

If it had not been for its constant strength of standing here tall for centuries, we may have never stopped. The roots of a young and not fully rooted down tree would have most definitely brought us to our timely demise, too caught up in each other. It is probably best that we did not die before we actually have the chance to indulge in each other's bodies and minds; not fully knowing what we had died for. Before allowing ourselves to find out, Romeo unmistakably thrives in this instant, allowing his hungrily deprived hands to make their way up my barrier of clothing. These very items of clothing are the only thing keeping our bodies apart at this very instant. The drive that leads them in their direction clearly shows the need and want he had been hiding so well from me. The warmth of his skin melting into my own. His touch, his lips electrify me in ways that I had not known possible. I sit up quickly, he follows suit. I yank his top off, the look of surprise on both our faces. *Am I really doing this right now? In the middle of the forest?* I place a hand onto his bare chest, leaning into him for another moment, lingering against his addictive lips, not wanting to let them get away from me before I have had a real chance to fully savour them. I twist my fingers into his hair, using this to pull him close to me, to fully feel his whole body pressed against my own.

"Ahem…ahem…"

Someone deliberately clears their throat to get our attention.

Romeo stands up faster than I have the chance to realise what is going on. I look completely frazzled. My shirt is lying across the dirt floor of the forest. *When had he done that?* I smile to myself remembering the feeling, until the person who had gone out of their way to get our attention asks me a question?

"Are you OK, is this man hurting you?"

That is when I too stand up, grabbing my shirt as I do, putting it back on, suddenly feeling very exposed.

"No, he is not, I started it."

I do not know why I felt I had to give them that information but I did. The woman look to me and notices the pink flush on my checks. Happy with what she has heard from me, and not worried about my safety, she goes on.

"You really should be more careful where you decide to lay."

Her checks that had been tanned in complexion now flourish a deep red, with what she had just said, not meaning it to come out the way it had. We both stare at each other then start awkwardly laughing.

"I am so sorry; I and my friends are hiking and seem to have gotten lost. You wouldn't know the way back to the docks? We are meant to be back in time for our tour."

She looks over to Romeo who had stayed very quiet throughout the whole exchange, probably extremely embarrassed from the way I had pounced on him, losing himself in the moment just as I had. He finally speaks up but makes a point to not look over to me, avoiding my eyes at all cost.

"Yes, I can walk you back down to the trail. I think you might have wandered off."

He gives the woman that irresistible smile, the same one he gave me when we first met. Does he realise the power he holds with that one simple gesture or is he completely oblivious to his natural charm and persuasion? I try to get his attention, without the woman noticing, but I fail as it seems Romeo is complacent to keep avoiding my gaze.

Is he angry with me? Did I just mess everything up before it even had a chance to begin? What even is this but a crush! We know very little of each other, all I know is that I feel safe with him, I have not felt safe since before the day my parents died in that fire. I look over to him, he is already overindulged in a friendly conversation with one of the strangers. One of the men to be exact that had been with the woman that asked for our help. They both seemed to laugh in unison, clearly comfortable, both falling into a mutual respect for each other, and sharing topics of common ground in conversation with one another. The woman that had ruined the moment between Romeo and me walks close by my side. I stay completely in my own mind, thinking of what I can do to have a chance to know what really is going on inside of that brain of Romeo's.

"If you stare at him any harder, you'll have an aneurysm."
I look up to the woman who had just spoken, breaking my concentration on willing Romeo to look at me, waiting for it

to work, wanting it too so badly so that I can simply apologise, so he knows I am sorry for making him feel uncomfortable.

"Erh yeah, you're probably right."

I kick a stone in my path, causing it to roll off the side of the hilltop we are now descending. All those winding roads and off bush tracks the taxi had taken to get here are starting to make sense now, as I look down and around the pulchritudinous mountain. We seem to be on the one to the right that stands large, letting the water flow freely between the two. The water below swirling around, taking with it the secrets of the day that have been.

I can just about make out where Romeo is taking these people we came across suddenly in the forest. It seems to be quite a touristy area, lots of people taking pictures, kids running. The parents are yelling for them to come back and stay far away from the edge of the water; well, that's what I am assuming they're saying, as we are still so far up that they all look like little ants running around an ant farm with nowhere in particular to go. I chuckle to myself imagining them as ants with their little legs and big heads running around like crazy, carrying things five thousand times more heavier than their actual size. How crazy would it be, if we actually got around on all fours carrying boulders upon our backs, lodging things around for actual ants, us becoming their mules just as we have treated donkeys and horses for generations. They do to us what we had to them. Oh, wouldn't that be just? Humankind finally getting a taste of their own medicine.

I come back to the present situation. I always end up getting lost in my own mind babble about the most irrelevant things to what I am actually doing at that very moment. Ranting and raving about things that I can do nothing about within my own mind but get angry at myself. I laugh again, this time louder, which evidently catches Romeo's attention, I watch as his head subtly turns around to catch a glimpse at what I could possibly be laughing at.

I take a chance to try to lighten the mood between the two of us as we are separated amongst the gang of people we decided to help back down this mountain. I go for a playful tongue game, sticking it out as far as I can, pulling a silly face, making Romeo unwillingly burst out laughing. He ends up snorting from trying so hard to hold it in, which makes me burst out laughing even more, throwing my head back trying to get control over myself. I look back to him with a necessity and desire in my eyes. I catch him still staring back to me; instead of a mask to hide his emotions from me like he had done seconds before, now lays a genuine smile, one full of mischief and promise.

I look down to the ground, a scarlet red rising to the tips of my cheekbones, remembering his lips against mine and not wanting them to ever leave my own. I look to see him quickly turn his face away from my ogling eyes, but not before I catch a glimpse of his cheeks reddening in response of my own flattery. Cleary feeling the need to get close to me, now realising the distance that has formed between us, wanting nothing more than to hold his hand in mine. To feel his warmth in my palm, to feel safe. When we are together, it feels as though nothing could possibly harm us. Well, that is how he makes me feel, I feel as though we could take on anything, and somehow come out on the other side stronger than we had entered.

I catch my footing quickly after I had managed to forget where I am supposed to be walking, nearly falling down the side of a never-ending cliff. Romeo's luring smile had distracted me from watching what I should have been doing. I'm quite happy to imagine myself being safe in his arms, forgetting to actually be safe from where I absent-mindedly put my own two feet.

We continue the rest of the walk down in relative silence, a few sporadic conversations shared here and there mainly about the view and how fortunate they had been to get lost on such a beautifully sunny day. By the time we reach the docks and say our farewells to the group of backpackers we had stumbled upon, or should I say they had stumbled onto us, quite literally, we evidently find out that they are backpackers, which we had found out amongst the random back and forth chit chat that they had travelled all the way here to see the

'South Island', big fans of *The Lord of the Rings* apparently. I also found out this is one of the locations they filmed in. Hence, all the tourists.

I have managed to work up a sweat walking down to the docks. I drive the back of my hand across my forehead, wiping away the residue that has accumulated there. I look to the ever-inviting water that splashes against the rocks I now stand on, looking out towards the two mountains on either side, the water playing amongst the boats and rocks. The sound of the waves crashing against the rocky pier seduces me to its appeal, the cold, wet water brushes my face, the taste of salt present on my lips. I lick it away. I take a step forward ready to indulge myself in its cooling liquid, soothing my muscles from the hike we had had, and readying them for the one to be had.

"Wait!" Romeo shouts over the roaring waves crashing around us, wanting me to wait before diving in.

"What? I am stinking hot; can we not stop for a swim for a little while?" I remove my top, leaving me standing in just my bra and shorts, I reach down to remove my shoes but not before Romeo interrupts me.

"Wait, I know the perfect spot we can go for a swim, somewhere more private, and with a waterfall."

The moment the word passes his lips, I am taken to his idea. A waterfall sounds absolutely divine.

"Lead the way then," I curtsy playfully, trying to add to the mood, not wanting him to revert back to the cold mask boy that had been directed towards me. It made me feel so little so quickly. I do not want to feel like that again.

Romeo catching onto the mood instantaneously grabs hold of my hand and picks up my shirt from the floor, leading me towards a wooden bridge, one that seems to be closed off to the public but that does not divert Romeo's direction, it only quickens his pace not wanting to be caught by anyone passing by. I giggle in excitement, loving the thrill of what is to come. We reach the gate to the bridge, Romeo hands me back my grey shirt, then leads the way, using the mosey bank to help get a leg up and over the tall metal gate.

A big yellow sign is cable tied to it, warning people away. Romeo gets to the top of it, then leans down to give me his hand. He pulls me up while I use my exhausted legs to push off the greenish-yellow hue of the mosey bank. We both jump down, landing in a tangled heap on the dirty ground, still obviously dampened by the constant stream of water running down the walls, leaving, unlike the other dried-up soil, wet.

Our clothing sticks to our skin. Romeo lifts up his finger and wipes it down my nose, leaving behind what I guess is a line of wet, brown dirt down my face. I wiggle my way out from under him, throwing a handful of mud that I had scooped up on my way, aiming it directly for his face but he is too quick, spinning around before it ever had a chance to hit its intended target. But he is not fast enough to altogether avoid it. There is squelching sound as it hits the back of him, it slowly makes its way down his back, getting caught in the top of his trousers.

"That's it, you just declared war."

He scoops up a handful of mud in his own large masculine hands. Running after me, as I had decided then and there to run for it, not wanting a mouth full of earth.

We continue running through the little wooded area before reaching the bridge. I stop to look up at the rocky face of the hilltop, water crashing down into the pool beneath it. The slightest rainbow appears from the water spraying around us. If you concentrate and focus your attention towards the mist, you could make out the faint individual colours.

"Is this it?" I ask, looking over to where we had been standing before, it does not seem that much more secluded than we had been over on the peer.

I can still hear and see people over by the water as they wander on down, gazing out at the view I had been admiring seconds before.

"No, it's still a bit further, this is just a small waterfall in comparison to where I am taking you," he smiles his winning smile, as he watches me taking in my new surroundings, loving every millisecond of it.

I look onto the boat that has been shipwrecked within the confinements of the waterfall and the bridge. I wonder if the people who had been on that boat thought it was a good idea at the time, until the water from the fall had waterlogged their little boat, making them abandon ship. There is a sign on the bridge warning people to not cross over with their boats.

I wonder if that was put there afterward. Romeo slides his fingers between mine, urging me to follow him.

I happily walk side by side. Occasionally Romeo has to stop and pull me up off the ground. After tripping over the roots in the uneven floor, it is clear this is not pathed for people to wander freely through.

I push back a fern that had overgrown, pushing our way through it trying to avoid the hit back. I peer my head up again after lowering it, not wanting to get anything in my eyes. When I do, I see the most magnificent waterfalls I have ever seen. The rainbow here is naturally easy to see, it stretches right across the lagoon, making it look as though it had purposely been put there.

The colours are so vibrant. The water droplets that continuously splash from its colour spectrum transfixes me to its unique beauty, if it had been made of hard material it could act as a bridge to the other side. While I still stand to gawk at the natural wonder in front of me, Romeo has stripped down to nothing, running past me straight into the clear blue water. You can see the bottom of the lagoon but as it slowly gets deeper the water becomes darker, until it is so deep the water is an almost blackened emerald green. I follow Romeo's lead, removing my clothing. I leave only my underwear on but throw my bra to the side with the rest of our stuff. I take a few calculated steps back and run for the water, waiting for the glorious moment; the calm cold water washes and submerges over my willing skin.

The water bubbles up around me, from the impact of the force with which my body hits the surface of the water, breaking it, allowing me to fall through its grasp. I stay submerged under its weight for a little longer than needed, looking around me at the wonder that is the world under this crystal-clear bliss. I slowly make my way back up for air, pushing my hands to pass my sides, using this momentum to bring me back to the surface of the water. I take a deep breath, filling my lungs with the unpolluted air.

"Now where were we?"

Just as I draw in a breath, my lips are plunged and taken over with Romeo's big succulent lips. The warmth I had craved before is now back where it belongs, my mouth falls into the kiss that had been rudely stolen from us. Before it has a chance of being taken away from us again, we dive in hungry, wanting more, needing more.

Romeo keeps his arms wrapped around my waist, keeping me warm as the sun begins to hide behind the trees, we are nearly back at the school. I notice this not a moment too late, stopping Romeo where we stand, nestling my face into his chest, not wanting to say goodbye yet. Because like many other schools, they have a strict policy about students being in other students' rooms after hours, especially if it is for something other than studying. He holds onto me that little bit tighter, also not wanting the moment to end.

"Do we have to go back?" I stare up to his whirlpool eyes, the blue mirroring the reflection of the lasting sky, just as the crystal-clear water of a whirlpool would.

"Yes, we do," he replies.

I reach up on my tiptoes to saver one last kiss. Romeo's breathing begins to quicken, matching my own laboured breath. The memories of the afternoon we spent in each other's arms down at the lagoon come forth. We had both undoubtedly got lost within each other. We had not noticed the sun going down behind the waterfall. We had been locked into each other's lips, only breaking to catch our breath. We had only explored every surface of the body of the other, never having the need to take it any further. Not that Romeo's and my first time together, underneath a waterfall, would have been the worst place to indulge in each other. We had both decided to take things slow, to get to know each other better first. It was not from the lack of wanting that stopped us but from the fear of rushing things, neither of us wants to ruin what we have before it has fully started.

"Wait till you fall asleep tonight, I will visit you in your dreams. I can only physically manifest inside your mind once it has hit rem sleep."

He gives me one last kiss on my forehead before heading in the opposite direction to his dorm room, probably commencing to the showers to warm himself up.

Wait till I fall asleep? He'll visit me in my dreams? What is that supposed to mean, does it mean exactly what he has said? I think this over, can he really mean that?

Not wanting to waste another second, I rush down the corridor into my room and straight into the shower, getting ready for bed. Once done in the shower, I rush to brush my teeth. We had missed dinner, so my stomach grumbles. I ignore it wanting to fall asleep, to see if what he said had been literal. Who knows with this place, I have seen crazier things.

My legs begin to tremor under his hypnotic stare. Staring into each other's eyes with a longing we could only begin to understand. Seeing right through each other's every need, want and desire. Sending pulses throughout my entire body, feeling things I have never felt before. I feel my body react to his in anticipation of what's to come. They are screaming now, telling me to rip his clothes off. To feel his warmth against my very own flesh, to feel the pressure of his pelvis as he begins to lean into me. Wanting nothing more than for this to be a reality, to not only be able to hold close to each other in our dream we share but to feel the closeness of each other's genuine warmth, as we had yesterday; his hot breath against my neck as he carefully places perfect kisses along my neck and jawline. Until reaching my plump juicy lips, eager to be touching his, to feel his tongue inside my mouth. Share more than just this dream; to share each other's soul and body in one.

My eyes flutter open involuntarily, instantly making my mood for today terrible. I turn over in my bed trying to get back to sleep where I had left off last in my dream with

Romeo. I toss, I turn. Again and again, growing more frustrated with each movement. Angrier at myself for waking up, but more so that I can now no longer fall back into that dream to finish what I had started. Annoyed, also realising falling back to sleep is out of the question, I unwillingly pull the duvet off and slide my legs off the bed; my feet place into my waiting flushed pink, sheepskin slippers.

I know I haven't actually had sex with Romeo but we have shared a dream of what it could possibly be like. I reluctantly stand up from sitting on the edge of my bed. Pulling up the covers, making sure I leave it looking neat before throwing on some none thought out clothes. Then, I proceed to fix my hair. *How should I wear it today?* I have not worn it down since the day I got here, maybe I will wear it down today, something different. Hopefully, it will make me feel a little better, perhaps even shift my mood a bit. While I'm already on this path, I think I might as well put some effort in for myself and decide to put some makeup on too. Once I finish, I look into the mirror. It is truly amazing what a little bit of blush, eyeliner, lippy and mascara can do for your mood. My hair looks good, I feel like a new person. Still slightly pissed off at myself for interrupting Romeo and my dream session.

But I suppose there is always tonight. With that, I head down to go to my first class. It is a training lesson. Back home, it would have been called physical education. But here it is called training because they are going to train me to learn how to fight and use my abilities apparently, so yes, I have most certainly never taken a class like this one before.

I approach the grand hall; the ceiling is a glass dome reaching over two hundred feet above us all. I take a step inside, my footsteps echoing off the walls as I continue to walk over to the group of people in the middle of the hall. All the students had just been in a deep conversation with one another, now all turn to face me on hearing my loud footing as I enter the hall. One of the students makes a smart remark,

"She is not going to last two seconds out there. Look, she cannot even enter a room without making a scene. Did someone say stampede? Or do they just simply mean, Victoria has decided to join us."

I hurry up then, wanting to hide in the group of students, no longer wanting to be in the spotlight of Sylvia's nasty comments for an instant longer.

One of the other boys from the group of friends Romeo hangs out with approaches me. At first, I think he is staring at someone behind me. As he slowly makes his way over to me, the students automatically move out of his way to create a pathway for him. Realising then that he is looking at me, I try miserably to think of something smart to say to him, once he has finally descended to where I am now stood. Just shy of the far wall of the hall, where I have decided to lean against. I stand up straighter then but misjudge my balance. I end up diving all over the place trying to keep upright.

Great! Real smooth, Victoria. Do you want to look any more a fool than you already do?

"Hi, I think you know my brother Romeo?" he breaks the ice first, coming in with something we may have a common interest in; interest is an understatement.

"So, you are his brother, how many does he have?"

"I am his only brother, younger, of course, and better looking."

I see the similarities then as the same smile inches its way over his face, they both share that mischievous look. Both oozing with confidence.

"We also share a younger sister together. Anything else you would like to ask while you are at it?"

His smile spreads across his face. As it grows, it becomes contagious, leaving me unable to do anything else than to smile in return.

We fall into a natural conversation, neither of us having to force it. The trainer enters the room. Then, everyone breaks up into pairs leaving me and Romeo's brother stuck together. *Great. What would Romeo say about this?*

"My name is Tane by the way, in case you were wondering."

He shrugs it off as if he couldn't care less, as he makes his way over to the corner of the hall to grab some mats and set out our circuit for training.

Fitness 101, according to this teacher, is to always be the fittest you can be at all times, so you will never be caught off guard. I suppose I need to get my butt back into gear as I have not been doing my usual activities, apart from some yoga to stretch out my sore muscles from carrying around the emotional weight of losing my parents. I haven't really been focused on keeping on track. I guess that is all about to change.

My attention is drawn back to where the teacher stands at the front of the hall, two students standing to one side of him.

"You will all be starting off with a set of eight, twenty-second intervals, with a ten-second break between each set. You will do this six times all the way through. Anyone unable to complete the first task will be made to do it again at lunchtime, and every lunchtime after that till they complete it, do you understand?"

He stares down each individual student, trying to strike fear into us. Half of the students chatter away about how easy it will be and about 1%, which consists of me, wish they could run and hide under a rock somewhere.

"Hey, do not worry. I got you," Tane's reassurance does little to make me feel better.

I smile towards him, trying to give him my most convincing smile.

"I thought today I would be learning what abilities I have and how to use them?"

My head drops down in defeat, feeling as though I will never have the chance to catch up with the rest of my peers.

"You will," Tane pats me on the back as he walks over to the matt, clearly going first to show me what to do.

I suppose I am just going to have to wait a little longer.

Chapter 6

I follow Ellie, the girl who is my roommate, now one of my friends here at this school, down the stairs at the back of the building outside, as we slowly start descending down into the forest surrounding the school. I take a moment to soak in my surroundings, taking in every detail of the breath-taking beauty the natural landscape offers. It is full of nature, the leaves on the trees rustling in the wind. The branches ever so slightly swaying rhythmically to the sound of their own music.

Ellie, who had introduced herself to me when I had been ready to give up and leave this place, not knowing why I had been brought here. I still don't but at least now I no longer feel alone in this place. I am grateful she decided to help me even after our little disagreement. We actually hit it off, we seem to have a lot in common, so I am looking forward to the adventures we will share together. She even offered to take me to get real answers as I had politely told her that even though she had been kind enough to go into elaborate detail about the history of the school we attend, it had not been what I had meant by need to know more.

Unlike Romeo, who only left me with more questions and nothing answered but he sure did make up for it in other areas. I smile to myself, remembering the two of us together.

I follow along beside her, thinking to myself that I wish I had decided to bring my jumper with me, in the end imagining it back in my dorm room. I picture the black soft material, feeling it against my skin, just lying there on my bed taunting me. Instead, I continue to keep walking deep into the forest, where the sun is no longer shining through and becomes darker, colder, and damper the further we go. A shiver runs up my spine and sends goose bumps all over my body. *Great!* Ellie looks to me then, realising that I am cold. She places a hand onto my forearm, then asks,

"May I?"

Confused by her question, I simply nod, intrigued by what she means.

When her hand is placed on my arm, it begins to almost glow a radiant warmth that slowly starts spreading up my arm and throughout my body. I feel warm but not just warm on the outside, but from the inside out. It feels amazing. It also fills me with a renewed energy I had not known I lacked moments before. Shocked, I slowly take a step away, releasing myself of her hold, not truly wanting to lose the warmth. I look up to her then.

"What was that? How did you do that? That was amazing."

She looks away from me, almost as though I had embarrassed her by the comment I made.

"Sorry I forget you are not used to these sorts of things. Don't worry, all should be answered for you soon."

With that she hurries along. I struggle to keep up with her.

"Hey, slow down. Not all of us are able to travel at such instant speed as you."

"Sorry, I'm such an idiot. Please forgive me," she spins around on the balls of her feet, to face me head-on.

"Don't be silly, you're fine. It's just me," I wink in reply, softening the tension that is evidently present on her face.

As we walk along the non-man-made path, we come across a barn out in the middle of the forest. It is beautiful. The wood is its natural self with a dark stain treatment covered throughout. There is a tree that has been built around to form the barn. The giant tree peers its head out of the front of the building, shedding its leaves onto the ground below, the ones remaining cast a weary shadow over the entrance, giving it an airy feeling, giving me goose bumps all over my body. *What is this doing all the way out here?*

Ellie answers my unspoken question.

"It's a barn, the tree is a kauri native to New Zealand, it is rare for one to grow in the southern part of this country."

Ellie looks up to the Kauri tree passionately, with clear interest playing across her facial features before she continues her explanation.

"They only normally grow in the northern region where it is warmer."

She looks down now, adjusting her clothing to straighten them out.

"That is why they have built around it, we believe it has spiritual properties that are connected to the land. They have been known to live for thousands of years. This tree has seen more in its lifetime than any of us ever will."

Getting back on track, she goes on to explain why we have stopped at this monumental piece of history that has been humanly preserved in the middle of the woods.

"We need to get off our feet for the rest of the journey, so we will be using the horses in the barn. Do you ride?"

"Do I what? I'm guessing you mean do I know how to horseback ride? And yes, I do. My mother taught me," I add unnecessarily in response.

I am forever oversharing when it really is not needed.

I look back up to the barn.

Who lives all the way out here? Why do we need to use a horse to get to where we are going? I begin to feel uneasy, not sure if I should go on.

I decided then, in that very moment of unsureness, that I should turn back to safety but as I do, a magnificent white horse comes walking out of the stables towards me, then nudges me with its head. What appears to be the horse's coat seems to be shining unnaturally bright. It looks like diamonds, as it shimmers under the lasting sun rays, casting prisms of light throughout the darkened forest clearing.

I stand with my delicate plump lips spread open in utter shock. I can hear a voice inside my head. I look around to see if anyone is near. Who could this possibly be inside my head, is it inside my head? I start to panic and grow more nervous, unsure of what is real and what is not. Then the voice inside my head speaks again.

"Victoria, it is OK. Calm down. It is me. Athena."

The voice is smooth like velvet, as it makes its way through my thoughts.

I look around trying to find who this voice belongs to.

"I am who stands in front of you, I may appear as a horse to you now. But I am many things, I will be what you need. I will serve you till the end of time for I am your familiar."

The horse throws its front legs up in the air, while thrashing its mane wildly through the wind, inches away from where I stand now. I look at the horse in front of me then. Staring straight into its eyes. As I do, I feel a connection grow between us.

What is happening? I am truly going insane.

I need answers now! I scream at the top of my lungs inside of my head, not that it is any good. For that, it is only inside my head. No one else is able to hear my cries.

Ellie looks to me then.

"I suppose now is as good a time as any. I was not expecting you to have a familiar already. I was never expecting it to present itself willingly to you either. You normally choose what you want but it seems yours has chosen you. Of course, it has to be a bloody horse of all things. We are only allowed household pets. I do not know what Mr. White is going to think of this. It seems to be out of your control though!"

Ellie turns away from me then, thinking over what she had been rambling on about seconds before. Seriously, I am going insane right now. Who cares if I have not chosen a familiar for myself but it has chosen me? That still does not make anything any clearer for me, or explain what the hell I am! Plus, I am not even sure it is a horse. Should I tell her the horse just spoke inside my head. No, I better not. She probably already thinks I am a bit on the strange side. Why add any suggestions to the flame, and how on earth does she know it is my familiar? I have not said so, unless the voice it presented me with inside my head was not actually just inside but projected to her too? But I am sure if it had been, she would have said so. Would she have not?

The blood through my veins begins to boil under my skin. I freak, thinking I may be falling into yet another uncontrollable panic attack. I am so sick of this; of everything. I decide right then and there I am no longer going to fall victim to myself any longer. I take a deep breath and let the feeling flow through me. Instead of fighting it and panicking, I welcome it. The very instant I have this revelation, everything changes. I no longer feel panicked, but the complete opposite; I feel complete.

My blood continues to flow through me, getting hotter every second. My skin on my entire body starts to radiate intense heat, like nothing any human being would ever be able to comprehend. The clothes that had moments before been hugging perfectly to my curvy, slender figure, melt into flames, then descend through the air as nothing but ash. Then, the unthinkable happens. My whole entire body bursts uncontrollably into what could only be described as a roaring flame, licking itself upon my skin.

Before I am able to react in any way, everything that I once thought to be me explodes within me and out to all that I can see with my naked eye around me.

Ellie goes flying backwards through the woods, at a speed you would think not possible, hitting a giant oak. Her body connects to the bark of the old oak tree, standing in the path of the chaos that has been unleashed upon it unjustly. An ear-cracking snap echoes through the woods, sending chills up my spine.

What have I done?

Her body folds into itself and crumples into a heap. It plummets its way to the ground, then lies completely still, showing no signs of life. I scream as I have never screamed before. The fire comes soaring straight through the hole that is my mouth. Passing my delicate lips and causing destruction all around me.

The whole forest, including the stable I had been inside moments before, is now engulfed in flames. The flames that are still being admitted from my very being. I turn to see a boy standing next to me, holding on to my shoulder, yelling for me to stop. I look into his eyes. I can see my reflection. My very own eyes are burning with luminescent blue flames. I close them then. Not liking what I see, I whisper into the air around me, suffocated by the smoke I have created.

"I don't know how!" Tears start pouring from my eyes but before they have the chance to fall down my fiery cheeks, they turn instantly to steam. I am crying steam right now!

"What am I?"

The boy, who is still holding onto me, tightens his grip. I do not know how he is able to hold on to me in this condition. He pulls me to face him then, and shouts through the thick smoke.

"Calm down, try and centre your thoughts. Control your emotions. Think of cold thoughts, think of the energy you share with the moon, on a full moon winter's night."

I close my eyes tight, zeroing all the noise around me out. Putting from my mind the scene that is before me, I allow myself to un-restrict my mind completely of anger at this moment, bitter hatred and frustration. I think of the snow that falls on to the mountain tops and settles down for the night. The wolves in the mountains playing in the snow. Howling up at the full moon of the darkest night.

Filling my mind with happy thoughts, visualising the fullness of the bright full moon. Within the chaos that is beginning to settle into a calm blizzard inside my mind, the moon sitting in the sky on top of the ice-cold mountains, preparing itself for the night ahead. Slowly, I feel my body temperature begin to cool down. A burst of energy echoes through me, then throughout the forest around me. Before I dare to open my eyes and look around me, I can hear the quiet of the forest once more, the sound of the roaring fire that had moments before taken over; now gone. I brave a glance up to look around me to see the damage I had somehow caused.

I look up then. I gasp in utter shock to see what had moments before been engulfed in flames, now completely turned to ice and snow.

It looks beautiful, like a charred, blackened winter wonderland. My mind goes to Ellie then. Picturing her body being thrown through the air runs horribly through my mind. I look around me, frantically looking to see where she lay. I finally spot her, about two hundred feet away from me, laying in the snow. I run over to her. Scared to see her body lying there, not breathing, not moving, no rise or fall of her chest.

I fall to my knees next to her limp body, tears now streaming down my face. I lean over her, looking to see any sign of life. My tears are falling now, rapidly down onto her charred chest, forming a puddle on her half naked body.

The boy who had helped me get control of myself kneels down next to her, on the other side. As he does, he places his hands over the puddle of my tears and begins to chant under his breath.

"Bring life to that was taken. Bring life to who lays here forsaken. Bring life to that was taken, for it was not to be on this forsaken full moon."

He grabs my hand to pull it towards him, placing it directly onto Ellie's chest, where the puddle of my tears sit on her burnt lifeless chest.

My hands begin to glow a radiant yellow, then does the boy's. Like the morning sun, its glow intensifies. To the point I have to look away, as it begins to burn my eyes. Minutes pass, maybe hours, before I hear the boy's voice call to me.

"Victoria, it is OK to look back now."

I cautiously look back to him then. Not wanting to look down, to see Ellie's dead body lying lifeless in front of me.

His eyes look into mine, indicating for me to look down. I hesitate at first, not entirely wanting to see what I had done. As I do though, I notice something different. The skin that had been burned to a crisp now lays in front of me pink with colour, clear from all signs of fire ever having touched it. It looks new, like soft baby skin. That is when I notice the rise and fall of her chest. Ellie's chest no longer stays still but rises and falls with life. Where once my tears had puddled upon her burnt flesh, now sit a detailed, beautiful heart shape. Encased in flames.

Ellie opens her eyes then, looking all around her before speaking.

"My head hurts, what happened here? The last thing I remember is feeling this crazy heat then everything went black," she stops for a second to evaluate her surroundings.

"Wait! When did it start snowing?"

I laugh then, happy to hear her speak, to see the blood rush to her cheeks in embarrassment. Thankful for her life.

Ellie puts her hand to her chest.

"What is this?"

The boy is the one to explain, as I do not know myself.

I continue to kneel next to where she now rests up on her elbows, confused, looking on gauntly. My eyes barely able to focus, my mind runs through the possibilities of what had just happened, trying to make sense of it all. I struggle to concentrate on what he has to say, wanting nothing more than to know what had just happened was not my fault or doing. It could not have been? Right? I stare dazedly, fixated on the details marking Ellie's new chest.

"I had to channel the power in Victoria's tears, through her hands, as she is yet to fully understand the extent of her gifts herself. I had to bring you back to life but I was only able to, as she can only bring people back that she has taken with her own power and no other." His voice rings true to his genuine actions he had taken.

I look over to the boy who had just saved my new friend's life. I am so grateful, I go to thank him, realising then that I don't even know his name. I hurry to ask, suddenly embarrassed with myself.

"Sorry, I want to thank you for what you have done for me. A complete stranger, but I do not know your name?"

He looks to me, then takes a few deliberate steps back away from both Ellie and me. Worried I had just offended him, I go to walk towards him. Just as I had thought I had closed enough distance between the both of us, his whole body begins to vibrate uncontrollably, feathers begin to cascade all around him. Where once a boy stood now a burst of exquisite feathers explodes from inside him, leaving behind a white, diamond coated horse.

Ellie looks to me, then back to the horse that now stood in front of us both. Then back to me once more.

"You have got to be kidding me, how is this even possible? I want answers now too!" she shakes her head in confusion, trying to piece together what she could not begin to fathom.

Then, just like before, a voice that had once been foreign to me, comes to me now, like a second conscience, it creeps like a stubborn shadow through my mind once again.

"It is still I, Athena, your familiar. I am to be whatever you need at any time. Whether it be a horse or a human boy."

I scream.

"ATHENA!"

Chapter 7

As we ride on horseback along the forest path littered with fire torches on either side, they flicker in the dark, casting shadows of the trees onto the path before us. I hear a noise in the distance, then another. An owl hooting, a branch snapping to the side of me.

A light sweat breaks out over my entire body. I begin to shiver involuntarily. I whisper, cooing in the direction to Ellie, who is walking beside me, as though she were walking outside on a sunny day, soaking up the sun rays and enjoying the view around her.

Do we see the same thing as each other? Certainly does not seem like it.

"How far away are we? We have been riding for hours, it is pitch black out here now," I scratch the back of my head, feeling as though something had crawled up my neck uninvited.

"Not far now, maybe another ten-fifteen minutes?" she grabs onto my reins, flicking them up and down to encourage Athena to fall into a trot for the last remaining part of the journey.

I begin to fall into the trot along with Athena rising up and down in rhythm with her. I scratch my forearm this time, feeling another unwanted guest decide to crawl along my skin. Again I find myself shivering, grossed out by all the insects and creepy crawlies outside tonight. I keep trying to tell myself that I am not afraid, that everything is OK. If anything, everyone should be afraid of me by the look of it. How is it even possible to emit fire from my very being and then miraculously turn it entirely around 180 degrees for then it to turn into ice, snow even? I look around then, watching as the snow still falls around us, drifting silently in the night sky. The snowflakes' complexion standing out from the dark shadows casting from the monstrous trees. The smell of fresh, crisp snow drifting all around me. I still have not seemed to learn how to turn this off yet, I do not have a big enough emotional connection to wanting it to stop apparently, that is why I am not finding it possible to bring the snowfall to a halt. That's why we have been hauling ourselves through not only snow but inches of thick snow courtesy of me. That is why the journey has taken us so much longer. I have lost count how many times I have apologised to Ellie for not only the snow but for the fire that had killed her and left our horse's poor legs buried under mountains of snow during the rest of our journey.

I have been endlessly going over in my mind, again and again for hours now, trying to think of some possible answers to make sense of what I did back there.

I thought through all the comics, books and movies I have ever read or seen. I have come up with a witch, fairy, perhaps vampire. Maybe even a mermaid! But none of them seem to really fit. None of them breathe fire like a dragon, none also have the ability to form a snowstorm on command. Not that I can remember, anyway, maybe they can. Who knows? One thing is for sure, I need to figure out how to use these gifts I have developed today. Then it hits me, it is these woods. They have done this to me, I need to get out of them as soon as I can. Ellie shouts over to me then, getting my attention.

"Hey, are you OK? We are here now. You can get off your horse."

She throws herself off her own horse then and begins to tie the horse to a nearby branch, leading to the clearing I now see before me. It is completely untouched by the snowstorm I had created. The moon shining directly onto the lake in the middle of the clearing, the moonlight reflecting a glowing light across the water. The ripples in the lake bouncing off each other, making it impossible to look away, putting me in a trance-like state. I feel the water pulling me towards it, begging me to take the first step. The moon singing in my ears. Telling me everything will be OK, the child of the sun and moon no longer needs to threat.

I too then jump from my horse. As my feet hit the ground, I feel the vibrations from the earth, the energy flowing through me, becoming a part of me.

I stop walking when I realise Ellie does not follow. I turn to ask if she is OK, if she is ready to come with me, to finally get the answers I have been looking for.

"Ellie, are you coming?"

When I see the look on her face, I ask again.

"Are you coming?"

She replies then. What she says next surprises me, I would have never thought I'd be going on alone.

"I cannot go any further with you on your journey to find answers, I have to leave you here now. You have to go the rest of the way on your own. Once you get past the guarded archway, make your way into the lake, the moon is at its highest point so you must hurry. Once in the lake, fully submerge yourself underwater, wait there for your answers. That is where you will receive them."

I turn towards the lake, frightened to be going on alone, not knowing what to expect. *Pull yourself together! You have gotten this far, there is no turning back now, do you hear me?*

I stop for a brief second. *Stop being so harsh on yourself, you have been through a lot these past few days, months even, give yourself a break, you are doing great! Just a little bit further and you will have made it. You will finally have all the answers you have been looking for.* After giving myself a small pep talk, I finally stop. Then, I gradually take another step closer, then another. Before I know it, I have crossed the archway, now making a quick descent to the water.

I stop to remove my shoes, then take my jacket and jumper off followed by the rest of my clothing, leaving me standing in the breeze in nothing but my underwear. At least if I take my clothes off now, I will have something warm and dry to get into after being frozen to death in this icy lake. *What is the point of this? Are they just trying to kill me off? I know, we will send the new girl into an ice-cold lake to kill her off.*

As I put my first right foot into the pond, a brisk wind picks up suddenly, it brushes through my hair, sending a chill down my spine. Before I have the chance to place my other foot into the water, a voice that is carried through the wind whispers into my ear, telling me to keep going, that it is OK. To take the next step, I whirl around. As I do, I see my mother standing there in a white flowing dress. Floating above the surface of the water, just over the far left under a willow tree, which hangs over the lake itself. She looks beautiful, the moonlight reflects off the water, making her skin look translucent.

Hang on, it cannot be her, she is dead. I watched the house that both her and my father were trapped in explode before my very own eyes, how can this be? How can she possibly be standing in front of me right now? Ghosts are not real. If they're, why has it taken her so long to finally come to me? To see if I am OK?

I stop my thoughts then, thinking back to my sister lying in a hospital bed back in England. Of course, she would be back there with her, if she had to choose, I would have done the same thing. But I would have at least come to visit sooner even if it was for a brief moment. Anything is better than nothing. I sigh to myself, telling my thoughts to quit it, *She is here now. That's all that matters.* I need to stop fighting a battle inside my head with myself, it is pointless. I will only lose.

She smiles at me, then slowly begins to fade away. As she does, I scream for her to wait, to stay a little longer. I run into the icy water trying to get closer to her, to stop her. The water begins to get deeper; I have to swim now. I look over to where she had stood, no longer seeing her there. Tears slide down my cheeks, falling into the lake.

I stop and paddle enough to keep myself afloat above the surface of the lake. I had not realised how far I had swum out; I had nearly covered half the lake's distance. I turn around to head back to shore but as I do, my mother appears in front of me, blocking my path back to the shore. She looks to me then, her eyes sad, not matching the smile she had placed upon her beautiful face for me.

"Stay where you are, you need to start swimming to the bottom of the lake to see what it is you have come here for. You have come too far, my sweetness, it would be silly to turn back now."

With that, she vanishes again. *Start swimming to the bottom of the lake? How long do I need to stay down there for it to work? How deep is the lake? Can I even hold my breath for that long?* I think this over in my head, weighing my options. *Is this worth it? I could die!*

Then I think back to what had happened to my new friend, Ellie, how I had killed her. Then somehow brought her back to life... The image of her charred body makes my mind up immediately. I do not want to hurt anyone else.

With that, I take in a deep breath, close my eyes, then dive beneath the surface of the water. I begin my journey to the bottom of the lake. *Will I make it?*

Chapter 8

My eyes flash open, awoken by the blinding light piercing through the water. What the hell? I start to thrash around in the water surrounding me, trying to make it back to the surface. How long have I been down here for? I must have passed out from the lack of oxygen entering my lungs! I look down to see the reason why I am unable to swim up to the surface of the water, my ankle is twisted, caught between some boulders under the lake. *How do I manage to get myself into these situations and how the hell am I not dead yet?* I reach down to try and break free from my leg being trapped, trying and trying again, failing more each time. I slowly feel the energy and strength leaving my limbs, making them become limp, dead weight, useless to me now. I scream, letting out the last of the oxygen I had left in my body. I drift in the underwater current, swaying rhythmically in the dancing light reflecting on the surface, forcing its way through the depths of the deep blues of the floor of the lake. Just as I slowly lose all consciousness, my mother's voice reaches out to me, urging me to listen to her.

"Breathe, Victoria, breathe," she's screaming now, her voice no longer sounds like a faraway whisper.

She screams again, even louder now, right into my waiting ear.

"Darling, open your eyes. Please, my darling, open them now. Rosie needs you. BREATHE!!!"

I gulp to try to take one last breath but my lungs are filled with water instead; my chest now feeling heavy. My body begins to convulse back and forth, panicking from the lack of oxygen getting to my brain. I whisper into the water, hoping that it is enough for my mother to hear, for anyone to listen to me, to help me.

"I am sorry, I cannot hold on any longer."

With that, I lose all consciousness. My body continues to sway, where I have come to rest in my final moments, trapped between the two boulders now acting as my tombstones, cemented to my own watery grave.

My body takes over then, doing the work for me, setting itself to autopilot as I am clearly not able to manually pilot my own self.

It pulses out a signal, sending a message to anyone that will listen, to anyone who can help. I am thrown backward, from the force of the power emitted from my very being, resulting in my head smashing against one of the boulders that have trapped me here shamelessly, stealing my life away from me.

The blow to my head makes my body involuntarily gasp for air, sending a shock wave through my body, surprisingly starting my heart again. This time, my lungs are welcomed with air pulsing through them. I welcome it, like I have never before. Taking what felt like my very first breath. I will never take the air I breathe for granted ever again. I allow myself to take a moment in appreciating the air I now feel in my lungs. I look around me, seeing that I am indeed still trapped under the icy cold waters of the lake with the full moon setting in the sky. *How long have I been down here for? How long was I unconscious for? How the hell am I breathing underwater, goddammit?* I reach down to my ankle, trying to free it, I fail again. This time, I take a breath of oxygenated water, Thinking of what I should do. I close my eyes, then letting my body feel through the motions I had felt before, when it had taken over sending out a signal to those I needed. So, I let it feel again, to feel for what it needs.

My hand automatically gravitates to an outstretched position, palm facing up, in the direct direction of the boulders placed on either side of my leg. With that, I take a deep breath, feeling a connection click into place. Just then, an ultrasonic vibration pulses through my palm, hitting the rock before me.

It moves it but not enough, so I try again. I take another deep breath in, filling my lungs up with water that apparently my body can filter through my lungs, oxygenating and turning it into breathable air.

The vibration pulsing from my palm hits the rock again, this time releasing my leg from its internal hold. I turn to swim back up to the surface when my mother's voice appears again, warning me.

"Do not turn back yet, my daughter, stay! Get your answers. You are safe now. You have passed the first test. Swim through the cave, it will take you to where you need to go."

Her ghost-like voice echoes through me, oh how I have missed her voice! The sound of reason, the one that was always there to help me when I needed it most. The voice that even now though she is dead, still guides me; the sound of my distant memories. Or is it? I look around to see if I can see her but I cannot.

She has once again been taken from me far too soon. An overwhelming rush of pain and sadness disables me more than anything I've ever felt before. How can one single individual feel this much pain from the loss of someone so close and so dear, taken all too soon and now cruelly taken again? How something so significant to oneself, like finding the exact definition for the word, but you cannot honestly know the meaning of the word until you have suffered from the loss yourself, and experienced all it has to offer? You have to go through it yourself to fully understand the meaning of suffering.

I try to pull myself together again but it is an exceptional amount for one person to have to deal with in a lifetime, let alone in this very moment of uncertainty; with one's own life on the line. Could it be me next? *Will I be seeing her sooner than I thought? I do not know if I can do this all on my own, am I strong enough? Wait, is this even possible for me to do? This whole situation is just crazy.* I keep having the same thought over and over again because this is such an impossible situation. How I have got here? I do not know. What have my parents done? What were their lives before me, and how well did I even know them? Did I know them? Or did I see the version they only wanted me to see? I guess I'm never going to find out now.

I know there's only one thing; one certainty: I must continue, I have to get to the bottom of it. If not for myself then for my family, for my sister in the hospital and for my dead parents.

I seem to be continuously thinking sombre thoughts to myself when I should be focusing on more important things at this very moment. *OK, that is enough, Victoria, stop thinking this way, you need to get your head in the game. You're thinking about things you have no control over.*

Should I continue? I might as well, I have gotten this far, I have died. I think? I can now breathe underwater, so why should I not get the answers I deserve to have? Surely, I owe that to myself.

I take one last look up at the shore, looking up at the setting moon, I hope Ellie is OK. *Did she see my signal?* With that being one of my last thoughts, I take in the beautiful view of the water rippling above my head, distorting the image I can see, and a piece of rubbish floating above me in the otherwise beautiful water. Unfortunately, it is not alone. It appears to be accompanied by many more pieces of plastic and waste. The pollution on this planet is getting out of control, if what I am about to learn can do anything to help save my world then I'll be forever grateful, as this planet is in dire need of saving, for us as people are destroying it slowly; like a disease, an unstoppable epidemic. So invincible, it continues to grow and grow, until one day it will be too late.

Even with the plastic pollution on the surface of the water, I still savour it for a moment, not knowing if this will be my last chance. Not knowing if I will make it out alive. I have barely made it already. *Am I strong enough to continue on this path of truth?*

With that, I swim more profoundly into the water that had tried to claim my life. *Am I crazy? Do I really have a death wish? I suppose I am going to find out.*

The water grows colder the deeper I swim into the cave. It becomes darker and harder to see, soon it will be as black as the night sky I have left behind on the surface, and all I will have left is the memory of the direction I think I should be heading.

I keep pushing forward, with the image of Ellie inside my mind, not wanting to ever have to witness something like that again. I hoped the darkness will help block the picture out of my mind but it has done the complete opposite. It's like it has harnessed it, making it as if it's happening all over again right before my eyes. I try opening them, needing to get out of my cruel head. Still, I can see nothing. Then all of a sudden, I see a glimpse of light, small at first. Then as I continue to swim forward, I can see the cave come to an unfortunate end. I panic briefly before I allow myself to look up. I then know the cave only changed direction instead of coming to an abrupt end, now heading upwards towards where the light had managed to break through the depths of the water, at the bottom of this dank, cold and dark cave. The cave that sits at the bottom of the lake I rightly fear, knowing it is haunted by the ghost of my mother.

I swim towards the opening, the light growing brighter the closer I draw nearer to it. I welcome the light but it burns my eyes, as I have been bathed in darkness for so long. I break free of the water, gasping for air that I do not need out of pure habit, welcoming the fresh breeze on my skin. I push back my hair going under the water one more time to get it out of my face. I make my way slowly to the side of the cave, where it sits in on itself. I look around me, then fully taking in what's there. I have never seen so many crystals in one place before, even the cave walls sparkle like a clear unpolluted night sky full of stars. I take a moment to look at the beautiful crystallised walls around me, not wanting to ever look away. If I could stay here forever, I would. I feel so much joy, fulfilment and hope.

A child appears out of nowhere, seemingly appearing to walk out of the crystallised walls, walking towards me, her eyes like the blue crystals that lay around the opening of the water. She walks over to me and places her small delicate hand onto my shoulder. Her hair, as white as snow, falls into long sheets down her back, almost touching the floor. Her lips slightly parted in a ghost of a smile, not quite fully forming a genuine smile, her hair flowing with the fabric that clings to her petite child body. The ashy blue silk cascading all around her making her appear angelic, or is she a ghost? A voice so calming, like flutists playing beautiful melodies, projects from her vocal cords but it becomes unbearable, the note becoming increasingly higher, hitting a C3 octave, without ceasing to stop.

"You will dream of what you are to come, you will see what it is you are to be. For that, only you can answer the question you most desire, and that is what you are. You're nothing that's been seen before, you're not what's meant to be, for your parents went against the wishes of their people. You should have never been. You are the daughter of the moon and sun. The granddaughter of the wolf and the lion; the child of the five earthly elements. The power you hold is unknown to all. Only you can find it through your quest of life, you cannot trust anyone for they want what it is you have, and those you find you can trust will only fear you, as they fear the unknown."

The little girl lets out a blood-curdling scream, then a pain shoots through my arm like it had been poked by a hot iron. I try to pull away but the young girl holds fast and does not let me go.

"We have agreed to help you as much as we can but you're to walk this path alone, as punishment for your parents' sins. We may not be able to give you all the answers now but we will send them to you as you dream. We will send you visions to help guide you on the right path but only you can choose whether you actually follow it or not."

Her voice grows quiet as she comes to an end, her eyes flash white as she screams again. With that a shock so harsh pushes us apart, throwing both the girl and me across from each other. It appears the blast sent her back through the way she came. I seem to continue to fall, flying back, hitting the other side of the cave wall. I smack my head against a crystal embedded in the wall. I instantly blackout from the force of the blow, and the stabbing through my skull from the black jewel in the cave wall.

I reluctantly open my eyes, regretting it the moment I do. The pain that is centred behind my eyes is absolutely causing havoc on two of my senses, those two being sight and hearing. The back of my head throbbing like there is no tomorrow leaves me in a paralysed state, not being able to move from the debilitating pain. I notice I seem to be rested on top of someone's strong, sturdy legs. I wince as I try to move, a voice tells me to stay still and advises me against it. I open my eyes more fully, reluctantly trying to focus in on what's around me. I see Ellie then peering down to me, her face covered with concern.

"Tori? Are you OK? You have been badly hurt. You're bleeding profusely! What happened to you down there?"

I try to move my head to the side to see who it is holding me, as it seems I am unable to respond with words right now. That's when the voice speaks to me again, calming and soothing as it is.

"Victoria, please do not move, you are seriously hurt. It is me, Romeo. I saw the signal you sent out for help. Well, I am not the only one who did but everyone else was told to stay put but I could not, as I knew it was you who needed help. I do not know how but I could feel it was you."

I can hear the shakiness to his voice, he sounds scared. *Is he scared for me?*

Ellie looks over me to him.

"How is this possible? Do you think?"

Romeo stops her before she can carry on.

"I have never seen this happen before, who entered the lake like many others have before her, to be welcomed and given their blessing. What made you bring her here now? You should have waited for the proper ritual ceremony, maybe this is why she has been hurt so badly by our elders."

He shakes his head back and forth while still trying to apply pressure to my open wounds.

"I am sorry. I thought they had told me to bring her here, maybe I was wrong. But I am never wrong," Ellie fights a battle inside her head, with what is right and what is not?

How could this have happened to me? Are the elders really that angry with me, with my parents that they would hurt me? They even refused to help me, to answer me! They refused to tell me who I am, only that I am to find out on my own, to walk the path alone.

What did my parents do that was so wrong? Surely loving someone cannot be all what they did?

I look up then, accidentally connecting eyes with Romeo, who had been watching every detail of my face looking for signs of me worsening. As we lock eyes, I automatically go to shy away but something stops me. It might have been the look of worry so evident on his face but the longer I look, it changes to something else.

The tension grows. It grows from worry to something I do not recognise. I try to make sense of the look that is now playing across his features. *If only I can know what is going on inside of that handsome head of his! Is he into me? He cannot be, why would he be interested in someone like me? I just see what I want to see. Could it be just my imagination? Or is there actually something growing between us? More than just a physical attraction we both clearly share for each other.* The longer I stare into his whirlpool blue eyes, the more I notice him staring back at me, not an inch of him wanting to look away. I don't want to break it but why does he not want to? Maybe he does like me more than I had initially allowed myself to think? Could the thought of him having feelings for me be that far-fetched? Why should I doubt he could possibly have feelings for me? Am I not worthy of having such feelings felt towards myself from another? He had answered to my call of help when no one else had. They had listened to the teacher's instructions? Didn't he say he could feel it was me, even without having concrete evidence he still came running.

That's when I felt the mood switch inside me. Yes, I may be laying here bleeding in his arms, holding onto my life but that does not mean I feel any less. If anything, my emotions

73

are heightened. I am more aware of what it is I want and feel, for I could lose everything in the blink of an eye. Right now, all I want is to stay lost in his eyes, for him to bring his lips closer to mine, to see what they would feel like against my tender and bruised lips. OK maybe it might be slightly inappropriate to engage in a kiss right now; for one, I might have blood all over my face. That is no way to bring our romance to life, through a bloodied kiss? Secondly, the timing is not ideal, and thirdly, I do not think I have the strength to move in for a kiss, no matter how much I may want one right now.

That's when it happens. I see the slightest movement in Romeo, as he leans forward, bringing his lips inches away from my own. I can feel his warm breath against my face, his eyes never breaking from mine. I hear a hitch in his breathing, it quickens ever so slightly. I can also hear Ellie pacing back and forth, still stuck with the turmoil inside her head. I feel I should say something to quiet her suffering. It was not her fault. She should not feel the need to beat herself up about it. Romeo must have become aware of her pacing too, as instead of placing his succulent lips against mine, he replaces the action with leaning his forehead into me, his breathing still heavy and laboured. As he does, he breaks our eye contact. My eyes flutter for a moment before closing entirely. I stay laying there in his arms, picturing his eyes inside my mind, memorising every ounce of detail from his angelic like perfection, saving it to my memory bank. I am starting to get a real collection of them from him, from the moments we have shared with one another. At least he has helped keep my mind off the current pain I am in, even if it is for a brief moment...

Chapter 9

Romeo's tone of voice changes drastically as my condition begins to deteriorate.

"Ellie, can you take us back to the school's medical department so we can get someone there to heal Tori?" he looks towards the horses hastily.

"Horseback will take too long, and will injure her further. You will need to try to transport all of us back."

This time he looks at Ellie then to me. I can feel his eyes lingering.

"I don't know, I have never brought that many with me before, I cannot take the horses too. Maybe, I can take the three of us back. I know, maybe I can attempt to send you two back together first, then I will follow behind. No, that won't work, you will probably both end up lost in limbo, as I need to always maintain a connection with you."

Ellie plays with her hands, unsure of her own strength and power.

I continue to lie in Romeo's arms, while he holds me close to him. Every now and then, he leans down to listen to my breathing, to make sure I am still alive. He has even gone as far to stop and check for my pulse twice. I lie there in a numb sort of way, knowing I should be feeling a lot more pain than I am right now. I do not think that is a good sign. My body must be in shock, every now and then the little pain I do feel spikes to an intensity that sends my body to unconsciousness.

I wake to the voices of Ellie and Romeo talking, again and again, discussing between them what would be the best-suited way to get me back to base. When I hear of Ellie being able to transport, I run through my head of what that means. If it means what I think it does, how come she had not used it for us when we had obviously struggled to come all this way? It would have saved us so much time, who knows? I may have never killed Ellie but I guess we will never know now as what has happened will remain as that, the unknown will stay unknown.

Well, that's what I think, until it hits me. A sharp pain spreads across the back of my eyes. As it grows gradually, it begins to prick at first, with what feels like individual needles running, trying to penetrate through the delicate skin that protects my sight, each one as though it was perfectly placed, creating a picture before my eyes as it tattoos out the image before me to see.

I see myself standing with Ellie and Romeo on either side. There appear to be three other people who I do not recognise, strategically ranked to either side of me, standing in the middle of a street with high rise buildings shadowing down around me. Buildings have been set alight, others completed demolished; all that is left is the rubble, to signify what had once stood tall. But one thing is made absolute, it looks like total destruction has plagued this poor unforeseen town into utter chaos.

In one hand, I seem to be holding an orb of fire, on the other hand it seems to be a radiant globe of water. As I look down to each one, the vision of myself does the same, looking to each of her own hands. I see my lips mouthing some words, trying to warn me from something but I cannot make out what I am attempting to say through all the static around me submerging my eardrums. All I can make out is the look on my face. I look scared, scratch that, I look terrified, but of what? I am screaming at myself now, urging for me to listen to her warning. I try to explain that I cannot hear her. I bring a hand around my ear, cupping it, to indicate I hear nothing. The static has shifted now, it sounds more like firewood crackling under the heat. I reach a hand out to her, wanting to help, to get her away from what frightens her so much, to get myself away from it.

Before I have a chance to save myself from the frightful situation, I see two of myself tragically trapped in. Everything changes, it shifts back to the blue sky I had seen once before, with the same pair of angelic eyes matching their background of blues looking down on me, to see if I am OK. *What was that? Is that what the Elders meant by showing me what they can? If that is true, I never want to see another one of those again.* A brisk shiver runs its course involuntarily through my body remembering how I had felt, the look on my face, the absolute terror that sat in my eyes as they looked to me, to warn me, to plead me to listen, to listen to what I could not possibly be able to hear through all the static interference. What was that I had seen? What had I just witnessed?

Romeo leans into me, whispering into my ear.

"You will be OK, Victoria. I promise I will not let anything else happen to you."

Shit, he used my actual name, how bad is it? I feel hurt but I don't feel like it is life-altering to the point it warrants the emotion that drips through his comforting words. The vast emotions that he carries through his words in regards to me, those same emotions I share for him. It's not like it is his fault, I got myself into this mess. Pretty sure I did that all on my own, also might be slightly my mother's fault too. *No offense, Mum, I do not wish to speak ill of the dead, as I very well know you are but seriously I am not, but why are you acting like you want me to be brought to my own untimely demise just as you had been? Seriously, what the hell, Mum?*

I decide to do a mental check on how different parts of my body feel, to try to gauge how bad I actually am. Do I really need urgent medical care?

OK, first, my arms. I try to move them to see what I can manage. I manage to bend my left arm. Not quite able to lift it above my feverish head. I think that's just more due to my muscles being exhausted from all the swimming and trauma I have endured. Now for my right arm, I go to move it but stop before I manage to make any real progress as a sharp, and rapidly progressing pain shoots its way through my lowermost part of my right arm, centred between my elbow and wrist. *Dammit, I think I may have broken it, maybe I am in worse shape than I originally thought.*

At that moment, I also realise Romeo had been talking to me. Too busy and focused on trying to figure out whether I am the world's biggest idiot for continuing into the cave after battling for air for God knows how many hours; I should have possibly just turned back. The Elders clearly did not want me there in the first place. Firstly, they refused to help as punishment for my parents' actions; again, my parents', not my own. I am being punished for no fault of my own, this is fair because? Anyway, the elders could not get me out of there fast enough, why would they send a young child to do their bidding too? Or was she an elder?

I must ask either Ellie or Romeo when I get the chance. I do not think now is really the ideal time. I think they are still trying to figure out how to get me back to school. Romeo is still talking to me. I think he is talking to me in a way that is to comfort himself. He is so sweet, his looks are out of this world—when I specify 'out of this world', I mean he is the definition of perfection on an encrusted gold-plated tray that only the royal family would be granted the honorary chance to be able to eat off of such an exquisite piece of art, they would be served the perfection of an angel. Is he an angel? Are angels even real? Who knows?

"You are OK, I have you now. Ellie is just trying to work out the exact coordinates to get us back to the school. She doesn't want to misjudge it and land us in the middle of nowhere, especially in your current condition."

Romeo is rubbing the back of my hand in a circular motion. It is strangely soothing. I think he decided to take hold of it when I had made the impulsive decision to prematurely move my arm around to see how badly damaged I really am; his way of telling me politely to stay still, I guess.

Ellie reluctantly interrupts my thoughts, as she begins to jump into the instructions of how we should prepare for her to transport us back to the school.

"OK, if we want this to go as smoothly as possible, I am going to need you to hold onto Tori still, keeping her close and steady to your chest. Have your legs bent, ready for impact, to minimise the jolt you will feel. I am going to hold onto your shoulders as your arms will be occupied holding onto Tori. OK, are you ready?"

I can only imagine the look she must have given him, as a wretched timed shot of pain sends me spiralling back into unconsciousness. It is probably for the best, as at that exact moment Ellie grabs forcefully onto Romeo's shoulders, sending us propelling back to the school.

We are met by a flurry of teachers who had been waiting in anticipation of our sudden arrival within the school's protective walls.

One of the teachers I had yet to meet—come to think of it I have only had one day of classes since being here, and I already have found myself in a hurricane of messes to end all messes—rushes over then, to see the full extent of the damage that has been caused.

The teacher shoots a warning stare towards Romeo, with a million and one questions playing behind her eyes, but she only asks one.

"Tell me what happened to her now!" Her tone sounds assertive but caring at the same time, she carefully takes me from Romeo's shielded arms, then placing me down onto a bed that sits in a row of ones that look exactly like the one I now lay on. This looks more like a high-end hospital ward then a medical centre in a school. There are about five beds in this part of the building, the odour mirrors that of a surgical room, the smell of bleach runs thick through the air, the clatter of busy hands echo through the preparation of machines being set up ready to be used on me to help stabilise my condition. That's when the doctor tries to divert my attention to him.

"Victoria, isn't it? I am just going to set up an IV drip in your preferred arm, OK? Then I will also be placing another needle, preparing your arm to be set up for a direct line to have the units of blood put back into your system that you have progressively lost, OK? This is crucial for your recovery."

With that, I feel a sharp but quick pain centred in the crease of my elbow. He works quickly with a precision of someone who has done this a thousand times before, his hands gentle and caring. I feel a second pinch on the top of the fragile skin that covers the outer layer of my hand as the second needle he had warned me about is placed accurately. He continues to tell me he is now going to administer a strong pain killer to help with stabilising the pain.

"You may feel slightly drowsy and not yourself after the morphine has kicked in."

He finishes up and starts to set the tray he had used to be cleaned and taken away. I slowly begin to feel the effects of the painkiller. It feels funny at first. I start to panic as I feel like I am endlessly falling down a deep tunnel, with absolutely no control of my body. I feel as though I am on one of those G-force rides, feeling dizzy and dizzier until I could throw up but before I have the chance to get that far, it all comes to a halt, settling into a beautiful calm peaceful wave, one that allows me to be entirely at ease with no pain for what feels like the first time in an extended concentrated amount of irreversible time relapses. I slowly start to feel myself drift in and out of sleep. Then, my ears perk up when I hear Romeo's voice. Just the sound of it makes me feel better, his voice sounding like my own personalised music made only for my ears, like they had been waiting to hear that tune all along, not knowing it was that they had needed to hear all this time.

"I told you already, I was not there when it happened. I only found her after she had gone into the lake. Ellie was the one with her, she had helped Victoria to find her way, and take her to it."

He runs a frustrated hand through his hair, making it fall into his eyes.

"Yes, I understand that you were not there but how did you know to go to her, how did you know where to go? Yes, Ellie is being questioned now about how our new student has been left fighting for her life in the very next room!"

She averts her eyes over in the direction I lay behind the carefully placed, closed curtain, assumedly asleep.

"It's hard to explain, it was kind of like a blinding camera flash, then when I went to go see what it had been, a line formed in front of me like a misty haze that had just appeared in the atmosphere from nowhere."

His arms now fall submissively down to his sides in defeat, like he knows what he is saying sounds crazy but he has to get her to believe it to be true.

"It kind of sparkles in the light, I don't know how. Or why? But I knew I just had to follow it. I just knew it was important. It pulled me towards it as if it needed me."

Romeo begins pacing now, growing more agitated and frustrated as each passing second feels like it's deliberately chosen to drag itself out as slow as it possibly can, to cause as much excruciating pain over having to wait to see if I will be OK.

I hear Romeo's footsteps become quieter after the teacher tells him he can leave and go to his dorm room to rest and wait for further questioning.

What more can they want from him, he has already told them everything!

That's when it dawns on me, they do not believe him. They think he is the one who has done this to me. Oh no, I need to hurry up and heal so I can clear all this unnecessary mess I have caused.

Body, why will you not heal already, hurry!

Apparently, the healer is away on holiday. Of course, he is. Why would I accept anything less than that in the first place? OK so the healer is off on holiday vacationing somewhere, probably enjoying sunbathing while I stay here unnecessarily suffering, for no other reason than that he had decided to take leave when I unmistakably need him the most. Of course, I know he was not to foresee the outcome of this tragic course of events leading me here.

I will need to do this the old-fashioned way, rest but not too much. I need to get back on my feet as soon as possible to help Romeo out. Who knows what they will do to him? I also need to do some physical therapy on my broken arm, what had the doctor said was wrong with me again? Something about a fractured skull that apparently has caused a haemorrhagic stroke, which can cause oxygen-rich blood to not be able to flow into the brain tissue, which can lead to Cerebral Edema. In other words, a blood vessel has burst to cause a bleed in my brain, which has resulted in minor brain swelling. Minor in the doctor's term, not with the way I can feel, my head pounding into the hospital floor beneath me and below. They would have put me into a coma but they had managed to get it stable enough, and under control; also my ankle is badly sprained.

I have a collapsed lung, probably from the force I hit the cave wall, which left me with a nifty gash across my middle section that they had to stitch up. I do not remember them doing this, so I must have been out cold. I do, however, remember every pull and twist as they placed my arm into its correct position for the cast. To say it was painful would be an understatement, it felt as though they had decided to place my arm into a pot of molten lava and then straight into an ice bucket, just thinking about it makes me tear up.

If only I had the power to manipulate time, this would be the perfect excuse to use it, to skip past all this dreadful waiting.

Chapter 10

I wake up still laying in the hospital bed, located in the school's medical building, situated on the far eastern side of the school grounds, not far from the stadium ironically. I wonder if that was done on purpose? They probably get a lot of casualties from there.

The smell of the school's idea of hospital food has woken me from my deep coma-like state. I feel awfully groggy this morning. It's probably from all the drugs they pumped me full of to help ease the extreme and intense pain I am still in. Not going to lie, it works.

Once I got past the first initial shock of the uncanny feeling, it's somewhat enjoyable, kind of like I had been floating on cloud nine all night long. I do not recommend the hangover you'll get the next day from the intense pain medication. Apart from the release of the pain, it's not all that it is cracked up to be. I would not recommend it, to be frank. I would not recommend getting in the situation I have gotten myself into in the first place.

I take a deep breath in through my nose, indulging in the wafting, lingering aroma from the food; my stomach grumbles in response. I did not realise how hungry I am until it wakens me. I cannot seem to remember when was the last time I had eaten anything at all. That cannot be good for my general health at all, let alone my recovery. How am I meant to get out of here quickly if I have not eaten? That's when I am brought back to reality about the daunting truth of what they could do to Romeo. All he had done was try and help me. Now, who knows what's going to happen? I lift the fork of food to my mouth, the beans running off the piece of toast as I aim it towards my watering mouth. The succulent butter melts within my mouth. You can never go wrong with traditional beans on toast.

That's when I hear it, a whistling and rustling as it steadily loudens like the wind has escaped from a cracked open window. Who the hell opened a window in here? The temperature drops drastically, setting a chill all over my body. Then in the corner of the room hidden behind the hospital's pale yellow curtains, where the noise had initially started from, footsteps now echo in the room, stopping just behind my closed-off curtains. I pull the bedding up to my nose, trying not to knock over my breakfast. Fear sweeps through me, what now? Then the curtains surrender to the unknown entity, opening to reveal one of Romeo's guy mates from his little band of friends. Relief washes over me instantly with the recognition. I think his name was Logan, if I remember correctly. I only heard it in passing conversation. I could be wrong.

"Victoria you have to get up now and get dressed. It's Romeo! He needs you," Logan sputters trying to get what he needs to say out. The urgency in his voice runs true to his word.

Romeo, as soon as the words leave his lips, I know it would not be good news. I guess my recovery will have to wait. With that I go to jump out of bed but I am stopped by the shooting pain across my abdomen. I try again, this time I ease my way up. Logan reaches out then to lend me a hand. He must have noticed the struggle I was going through just to get out of bed, I am yet to try to walk.

What about dressing myself? I cannot ask that of Logan, I barely know him.

I signal for Logan to grab my clothing that had been left on the red leather recliner seat beside my bed. Logan lifts an eyebrow in response, probably thinking the same thing I had just moments before.

I make a point of taking the clothing from his grasp, pulling the grey woollen jumper over my head, leaving it placed around my neck. I clear my throat, in indication for Logan to either turn-around or to stand behind the curtain he had just made his entrance through, so I can proceed in the impossible task of getting myself dressed.

It is already going to be debilitating, let alone with an audience's looming stare, criticising my feeble attempt of doing it on my own.

Logan gets the hint instantly, turning around faster than is needed. In doing so, he loses his balance slightly but he is quick to correct himself, with precision so precise it is not like anything I have seen before but I guess I should be getting used to that by now.

I stare at him in wonder, genuinely seeing him for the first time; there is still so much I do not know about everyone at this school. After I try and save Romeo, I need to make a point of getting to know everyone. If not to gain knowledge but to put into gaining allies.

I remove my hospital gown slowly, not wanting to disrupt the carefully placed stitches along my bloodied abdomen, that's all I need is for my stitches to open. I slide one arm through the first sleeve, then followed by the second, not bothering to attempt putting a shirt on as well. We do not have time. Luckily, I already have a sports bra on.

I shuffle clumsily into my jeans, hobbling on one foot. I grab one of my crutches that have been placed deliberately by my bedside, ready for my use.

I look up once I have somehow managed to calculatedly navigate my way into getting dressed with minimal pain inflicted onto myself. A little smile plays along my lips pleased with the outcome; I see a smirk on Logan's face as he turns around to have a look at me.

"You managed OK then?" he smirks to himself, trying to hold back the laughter.

"Yes, I think I did quite well considering… What's so funny?" I lift an eyebrow to show my lack of patience to hear what he has to say for himself.

"It's just that I have not heard someone shout so many profanities while getting dressed, let alone openly congratulating themselves for completing the task," he shrugs his shoulders to try and imply that he does not care either way.

"Again, like I said, I thought it would have been an impossible task, so yes, I was a little pleased with myself."

I pick up the other crutch and position it in the other arm ready to get going.

"Just saying you are a unique individual, Miss Luna-Maddicks, that is all."

Logan grabs the bag which has my stuff packed inside it. Ellie must have put it together for me. Then, he walks forward and opens the door waiting for me to wobble my way over, to allow me to exit as gracefully as one can while hobbling along on crutches.

As we make our way down the corridor, me following Logan's lead, I have yet to learn my way around the school grounds, due to all this erratic nature that has taken place. But he is more than happy to do so. Logan seems like a sweet soul. He offers to carry me every time I stop to adjust my hands from the pressure they are being put under to take my full body weight, considering one of my arms are in a cast.

I think he feels sorry for me, as my leg seems to be out of commission for the time being. Plus, the constant tugging at my stitches does not help the journey along. If only I knew, or had the power to heal myself, that would be more than helpful right now. Because all I am suitable for at the moment is slowing down the rescue mission to save Romeo.

"Where are they keeping him, do you know?" I manage to get out with little to no struggle, while I hurry to keep up.

"They are keeping him under the school. He is surrounded by guards, one of which can cancel out anyone's unique energy signature that gives them their abilities," Logan stares at me, trying to get across the severity of the situation.

"So, we are going to have to do this rescue mission the human way."

A weary frown creeps along his face, while he tries to cook up a plan, having to factor in the fact that his sidekick, *moi*, is still critically injured. A lot of help I am turning out to be.

"I can do that, I still feel human, I think like a human because I still have no idea how to use my abilities. I have yet to learn how to use them, or incorporate them into my daily life, so at least I can be of some use."

Surprisingly, I start to feel some hope, maybe it's a good thing that I am yet to understand all of this entirely, perhaps being clueless is the key we need to save Romeo, after all, who would have thought?

"Yes, that is perfect, we can use that to our advantage. They will never see it coming. They will be expecting all kinds of various energy signature attacks, because that's all they have been trained to defeat," Logan claps his hands together in a new thrill of adrenaline coursing through his veins.

"OK, here's the plan. You are going to walk up to them, in your current state they will see you as no threat, while I go check out the surrounding area and see what it is they are planning to do to him. You have to try to get through them so you can get to the leaders of K.K.R.R, before they can send him to trial with the K.R.R present, waiting to execute the trial. You have to explain to them what happened and clear his name as soon as possible. You will also have to prove that you are in your right mind; otherwise, they will not take what you have to say seriously," he stops then, resting his hand on my shoulder, looking deep into my eyes.

"Can you do this?" His eyes are pleading with me to understand, hoping I want to save him as much as he does.

"How do you know he is innocent?"

I look back into his caramel eyes with flecks of gold splashing through the sticky, smouldering colour placed perfectly on either side of his nose, his dark skin illuminating the intensity of them more, they advert my attention momentarily. Now only realising the closeness of our stance and only seeing him for his beauty now, for the first time since expeditiously on our quest to Romeo, for his safety. Does everyone that goes to this school have to go through a modelling agency before being accepted? I have never seen so many beautiful people in one place. He takes a step back then, unsure how to answer my question. He had clearly not been prepared for me to ask. He begins walking again, so I follow suit. Waiting for my reply.

"I have the ability to see into someone's thoughts, I cannot get a clear reading but I can feel my way through them, and I can tell if they are pure or tainted. I looked into yours while you were asleep, I could feel your want, need to get better and to help Romeo. I could feel your desire to make everyone know what really happened that it was not Romeo who had harmed you."

He braves a quick glance back to me to see if he can gauge my reaction to the news he has just told me before continuing.

"I'm sorry, I know I should have asked you first. But you were asleep, and I really needed to find out the truth as fast as possible so I could help my brother. I admit I was angry when I first came into your room, I hated you for what you condemned him to. I thought to myself, how could a girl no one really knows have caused so much damage in such a short space of time?"

He stops to take a quick breath, peering to the side of him, still trying to see what I thought of the violation of my privacy.

"But as soon as I peered inside of your thoughts, I knew straight away it was not your fault, and that you only had pure intentions. For that, I am sorry," he gives me a sheepish grin, hoping it would be enough for a peace offering.

"I hope you can forgive me."

Logan takes in a deep breath in anticipation.

I think this over in my mind, he has just admitted to hating me, then going through my thoughts and feelings? Is that what Romeo can do, my emotions always change so much around him. I did not know Romeo had another brother; they look a little alike but yet so different.

Who am I to judge, I killed, then brought back to life my new friend room-mate. He was only trying to get the truth, so he could help his brother.

Wouldn't I do the same for Rose?

"I forgive you."

I look back up to him with a reassuring smile placed deliberately on my face to soothe his nerves, he has been nothing but helpful and honest with me since, so I have no reason to doubt him.

"Really?" Shock clear across his face, he exhales as though he had been holding his breath this whole time.

I laugh at his reaction, the tension in the air subsides immediately, replaced with one that shows mutual respect now between us.

"OK, now that we have that all cleared up, how far away are we?" My mood changes to a more serious one, knowing what I will have to do next.

"The entrance you are going to take to enter the underground is just over there. I will take you to it but you will have to go the rest of the way on your own. I will take the entry point on the further east side. I will come and find you when the time is right."

Logan points in the direction we are headed.

"Try not to injure yourself any more than you already have, or at least wait till the healer is back."

He laughs that last part trying to ease my fear, and maybe his own too.

We walk the rest of the distance in silence, I can hear every little thing as if my senses have gone into overdrive. The light breeze brushing past the trees also sways each individual blade of grass. I can listen to the sounds of birds in the trees, along with other students out on the far-field training, utterly oblivious to what is happening beneath them.

My breathing grows heavier the closer we get to the secret door craftily hidden behind a row of bushes that decorate themselves along the outer wall, surrounding the headquarters of the school.

My stitches along my abdomen make themselves known, creating an agonising pain, ripping right through me. Not allowing me to forget what condition I am in for a moment longer. I try to keep going, ignoring the pain shooting its way through me but I trip and stumble on a rock. My crutches hitting it clumsily. I had been focusing too much on ignoring the pain, I forgot to watch where I was hobbling along. The crutch in my right arm stops and pushes my arm backward at an unnatural angle. A little shriek escapes my pained lips, as I reluctantly fall to the ground, crumbling at its mercy.

I shout profanities again and again through my mind, cursing my ignorance. I now lay sprawled across the lawn meters away from my destination on the damp, wet grass. I had not realised how slippery the grounds had become while I had been laying in the hospital bed. It had clearly rained. I secretly welcome the cold oozing from the earth, soaking it in as much as I can, the earth's cold temperature soothes the antagonising fire that continues to rip through my core that had caused me to fall victim to the earth. I place a hand against my middle section to evaluate the damage. I bring my hand up to my face to get a better look at what the warm liquid attached to my now raised hand is. I can now feel it running seductively through my fingers.

My hand is undeniably drenched in my own blood. *Great!* I cannot even walk to the tunnels, and I am already bleeding profusely all over the place, how do I expect to save Romeo in this godforsaken state?

Logan hastily walks back towards me, after turning to see what all the commotion had been he had heard going on behind him. Not realising it had all been me. He carefully crouches down beside me, careful not to jolt me, preventing any further bleeding.

"I thought I told you to at least wait till the healer is back before you cause any more damage to your person."

He looks over me with a precision that could only come from intense training, what does he do? Possibly a student here? How does he know so much about the tunnels? Does he work for the so-called K.K.R.R? I should probably find out a little bit more information about him before I go into unknown territory?

"What does K.K.R.R stand for?" I search his eyes for a clue, for any indication. I notice a slight change in his stance, his eyes become harder around the edges, he becomes instantly more guarded.

Logan looks away then, not wanting to meet the look of scrutiny in my eyes.

He collects himself quickly, thinking of a way to describe it without giving up too much intel.

He takes a breath and turns back to face me, making the decision then and there that I should know the whole truth.

"K.K.R.R stands for *Kawanatanga, Kei a...mō te...Rautaki, Ratonga*, which means Government Gifted Intelligence Service. We work under the Kawanatanga Rautaki Ratonga," he looks at me to see if I'm still following. When he sees I am listening to what has been said, he carries on.

"The Government Intelligence Service does not actually know where our school is located. Or what we actually can do. All they know is that we are extremely gifted, they think we are trained from the moment we can walk, that is why they think we are such gifted individuals. In all things combat, we tell them what they want to know. We call ourselves *Kei a...mō te...Rautaki*, Gifted Intelligence. It's a lot easier to digest."

He laughs at an inside joke that I am clearly not a part of.

'We call ourselves the Gifted Intelligence', I am guessing by the 'we' statement he is a part of the organisation.

"So, when you say we, do you mean you work for the Government?" I press my hand back down on my stomach to hopefully ease the pain I am going through.

Logan sighs to himself.

"Yes, I work for them, I was recruited last year."

I take a moment to let this all soak in. While I do, Logan leans over me, moving my hand out of the way, to assess the damage. He frowns into himself, placing his hand on to the wound, to apply pressure to help stop the bleeding.

He looks around to see if anyone has noticed the little scene playing out on the school field. I would really suck as a spy; I am pretty sure I have already compromised our position but lucky for me it looks like nobody's around to witness the carnage.

I fold over into the earth beneath me again, as another wave of pain shoots through me.

"I should take you back, you are in no state to even be walking. What was I thinking?"

He swears under his breath, annoyed with his own stupidity.

I breathe in the earth below me, welcoming the earthy scent, it feels so familiar to me. I focus my senses into the soil, letting the smell and the earth coat itself around me.

Logan stands up abruptly, taking a few hesitant steps back. I ignore him, as the pain I had been feeling begins to subside, I continue to focus and draw the earth towards me, noticing the effect it is having on me, a warm feeling washes over me like a warm summer evening's setting sun.

The pain is nearly completely gone, I look down to where I had been bleeding from my abdomen. I gasp in shock when I notice my whole body is radiating in a yellow, gold shimmering hue.

"What is happening?" I ask the question to nobody in particular.

I lift my jumper up to look at where the warm feeling is radiating from. I notice the bleeding has stopped. I make a closer inspection, then right before my eyes, the stitches one by one disintegrate into nothing, leaving behind the rejuvenated skin. I can still see where I had been hurt, only instead of an audacious scarlet gash that had been gushing blood only seconds before, now sits a fresh pink scar. It should not look like this yet; it takes weeks, months even before new skin begins to replenish itself. I run my shaky, unsure hand across the pink line now placed along my middle section, feeling the need to touch it to make sure it is real. *I wonder,* I think to myself. I look down at my ankle and reluctantly flex it, shocked when I am not rewarded with a blast of shooting pains up my leg. I continue to flex it. I get so carried away I stand up and start jumping up and down on the spot, I feel amazing. How can this be? I jump and skip around in a circle like a child let loose on a playground, so pleased with themselves for finally finding their feet.

That's when I look up at Logan, momentarily forgetting his presence.

"You are glowing." It was meant as a statement to himself, a way of him trying to come to terms with what was happening but I answer him anyway.

"It does seem to appear that way, does it not."

I am beaming now, my smile reaching as far as it possibly can, landscaping itself onto my all too willing face. *Did I just heal myself, how though?*

I look down to the earth under my feet, realising then, I had drawn the energy that connects us all from the land we walk upon.

"Thank you."

I let my thank you be carried through the wind, making the earth know how grateful I am for lending me its ability to heal, even just for a moment. I take a step back and look all around me, only now truly seeing the world for what it is. I can see all the energy passing through, around and together, connecting and making up all that there is around me. Each thing has its own unique spark. They dance and play, singing along, making them flow perfectly and rhythmically together, creating a show of light so perplexed. There truly is no word to describe how remarkable its illicit raw power is. With disbelief being my forefront emotion towards the show that is being shown to me now, to someone of my stature, I genuinely am not worthy or admirable enough for such a display of power, someone like me, dishonourable compared to the mighty earth's will. I should not be so lucky to be presented with such an open screen of their immense power.

I look to Logan to see if he can see what I am so clearly seeing in front of me right now but it seems he does not, as all he appears to be doing is staring right at me. If only he were capable of seeing what I am seeing, he would be looking anywhere but at me.

But all I can see now when I look at him is his energy force connecting him to his environment, merging as one. We really are a whole entity, each individually connected together through the energies that flow through the air we breathe and the ground we brace ourselves upon. Every movement he makes creates a new energy path that connects with a different thread of the universe's vast elements; energy force. He is a golden caramel, sparks of the gold energy flow from him, and is dispersed, being absorbed back to where it had come. I look a little longer than one should, taken aback by its raw beauty, the true naked form of Logan I see before me.

I can finally feel and connect with the power that flows freely through me, for I am the energy's blood source that combines all energies, they rush through me to become whole.

I am the heart of the universe, the power of all forces pump through my veins, restoring balance once again.

Chapter 11

Logan continues to stare right at me like he has just been mugged by a stranger in an alleyway, which turns out to be a dear friend.

"Victoria, you…you are glowing, no, it looks like you have multiple different electrical currents flowing through you, lighting up your veins. You are lit up like a firework!" Logan's eyes are as wide as bowling balls, his mouth not far off.

I look to him, reluctantly drawing my attention away from the beautiful world around me, seeing it for what it truly is; all the energies flowing through each other. I now feel as though I can begin to get a hold of these powers I have, it feels as if they have been awoken from a dormant sleep.

The little girl's voice runs through my mind, with one thing she said in particular, standing out.

"Do not trust anyone."

I think this over, before answering him.

"Logan, I do not understand what is happening to me right now. I feel amazing but I do not know why."

I watch as the colours that make up who Logan is, shift in tone, they become more stagnant.

I prepare myself for his reply. A look of confusion crosses his face.

"Logan?" he whispers this under his breath, sounding confused.

"Sorry, what was that? I did not hear you?" I put a hand to my ear to help indicate that I was unable to hear what he has just said.

He's quick to reply.

"Nothing, I was just talking to myself. Well, you must have unlocked something when you drew your power willingly from the earth to heal yourself."

He looks me up and down taking in my now uninjured body.

"How do you know it was the earth I drew power from?" I become guarded by this statement.

"I only assume this, as it was where the glowing originated from, drawing itself up from the earth and on to you."

He lifts his arm up playing with his man bun on top of his head, taking it down and redoing it again and again. He clearly does this a lot when he is unsure or trying to think something through. OK, I suppose that is a rational explanation for why he would think that. I need to relax.

"So, what's the plan now, we need to get going."

My mind coming back to the reason for us being stood in the middle of the school grounds. My crutches lay chaotically on the lawn, where I had been only moments before, in no fit state at all to be going on this mission, let alone be out of my surgically clean hospital bed but all that has changed in a blink of an eye. I now stand here perfectly OK, more than OK. I feel bloody brilliant.

"I do not know; everything has changed now."

Logan begins pacing back and forth, still puzzled and confused on how to continue forward with the plan we had set in motion.

Logan shouts unexpectedly, making me jump.

"Bloody hell, what is it?"

Annoyed for being caught off guard, I snap back more harshly than I intend to.

"You can still play the damsel in distress, only now, you are not. So, you can actually protect yourself, go up to the guards in the tunnel on your crutches acting as though you are still harmless because they won't know you can heal yourself. So why would they question it? This is going to work in our favour, more yours than mine. At least now I won't have to keep worrying whether or not you are OK, and not bleeding all over the place."

Logan bends down and picks up my crutches. Handing them to me, he then grabs my arm and starts pulling me along.

"OK, I get it, we need to get going but can you please let go of me? Plus, shouldn't I be using my crutches for it to be believable?"

I shoot the question at him, waiting for him to release his hold of me.

"You are right, sorry," he pats my arm where he had been holding on to. He shows his compassion and apologises, making sure I understand how sorry he is for not thinking before doing.

"Sorry, I should have asked your permission before touching you, I am sorry."

He bites his lip, all I want to do is reach up and touch it, to see if they feel as soft as they look. But of course, I do not do this, as it is inappropriate, also, I have feelings for his brother, the one we are currently on the way to save.

"That's OK."

I start to hobble along on my crutches, now realising how much of an inconvenience they really are, now that I do not actually need them. We continue on to the entryway in silence, both lost in our own thoughts. What should I expect? Will they be kind to me? Or am in for a whirlwind of trouble? I guess I will find out.

I look up, as Logan pulls back some branches covered in an array of greens like someone had decided to use all the colours available to them and transfer them to the leaves.

"OK, this is where I leave you. Are you going to be OK on your own?"

The look in Logan's eyes show a longing to stay but he knows too well that he cannot.

"I don't really have a choice now, do I," I give him a half-hearted smile, which he returns.

"Goodbye, Victoria Luna-Maddicks, I will see you soon." With that he crouches down and lunges himself on top of the building with ease, I would typically have been surprised by this explicit inhuman action, I suppose it is becoming normalised to me now if that is possible.

I look at the door before me, it is well camouflaged, the colours of the entry matching the surrounding area. I push against it to open it, only then realising the full weight of the fully armoured up door. I struggle with it, not getting anywhere fast. *Dammit, I should have asked Logan to open it for me. I am not strong enough. Unless?* I wonder, a thought comes to me, with the knowledge I now have. What if I draw the earth's energy towards me, to open the door? To use the added strength needed.

I take in a deep breath and clear my mind, only focusing on the sounds of the earth beneath me, allowing the energy to entwine with my own. I feel when the connection is made, this is it. I push on the door with no time to waste, not sure how long the link will last.

The door bursts open, shocked by the force I was able to apply to the object before me. I really should be more careful; I do not want to draw any unwanted attention my way. I look behind me before entering. Once past the threshold, I close the door securely behind, making sure no one can follow.

I do not know what I thought I would expect the tunnels under the school to look like but it was definitely not this. I pictured damp, wet walls, covered in mud and mould, with an endless stream of cobwebs lined out in front of me. I thought I would have to battle past giant spiders that had been left to grow untouched and undisturbed. I thought I would have been welcomed by a river running its course, soaking me through to the core. Witnessing rats swimming past me, to get to where they needed to go. But no, this is not what I see before me.

I see a long, extremely high-ceilinged corridor, outrageously white. It looks so clean I could eat my dinner on the floor. I look down a little further, trying to navigate my way down this endless tunnel, only to notice a giant metal door that looked like it was built to withstand a nuclear bomb. The lights here are a blinding fluorescent white, the dim light outside had not prepared my irises for this harsh reality. I notice the two guards by the door before they see me, they are stood either side. Oddly enough they do not stand armed but I guess if anybody needed not worry, it would be the people at this school, they have their weapons personally built into them.

I also notice a scanner on the wall, with a hand reader. Maybe even an iris scanner but I will have to get a closer look to be able to tell.

I deliberately take my time, hobbling down the long tunnel on my crutches, acutely aware that I no longer need them. This makes me nervous. What if they can tell I don't actually need these? Good thing I had put the moon boot back on, plus the cast on my arm. I still have the dressing across my stomach, where my wound had been. Should I make them aware of my presence before they notice me first? Should I call out to them? Pretend I have been sent down here, and that I need their help to get me to where I need to go? Oh my, I don't even know where I am supposed to be going? How am I meant to convince them that I do?

OK. I decide at that moment I am just going to wing it and hope for the best. I think if I am the one to make myself known; I might have a better chance. Here's hoping.

"Excuse me, can you tell me where I should be heading for the trial, I am a witness. I cannot say for what but I was told to ask you two for directions."

Oh no! Who in their right mind would believe a word I just said, I have messed this up already, why did I open my mouth? Bloody hell, Victoria! A light sweat starts to break out on the back of my neck. *OK, calm down, you do not want to give yourself away, calm down you're fine. You have obviously injured yourself, what's the worst they are going to do to you?*

"We have not been informed that someone would be sent our way, what is your name?" The guard to my right is the first to talk, the other changes his stance from casual to formal, getting ready just in case.

"Sorry, I should have said, my name is Victoria. I am a new student. That is probably why you have not seen me around before."

The guard on the left quickly shoots the other guard a warning stare, instantly recognising my name, the crutches probably helped clue him into who I am as well.

The guard to the right continues to act oblivious.

"Victoria who?" he starts to walk towards me, closing in the gap, the other one stays behind still guarding the entrance.

"Victoria Luna-Maddicks."

I slow my pace down, even more, trying to come across as exhausted from having to make my way down this endless tunnel.

The guard stops, the emotion changes on his face but he is quick to control it. What he does next truly shocked me. Nothing could have prepared me for this.

"Victoria, I am so sorry, here, let us help you. Max, come here now and take her crutches for her, while I carry her to the office."

He looks back impatiently to the guard whose name is Max. He looks a lot younger than the one who has just offered to carry me. He seems about Logan's age. He has a mop of curly hair laying playfully atop his head. With eyes so dark they look almost haunted but I can see a hint of green trying to escape the dark oboist.

"Sorry, sir," he begins a light jog as he comes closer, he waits for me to hand over my crutches but I just stare at the both of them, shocked and not sure how to proceed. Come on, this is good. We could not have asked for a better outcome.

The older guard looks to me, curious to my hesitation. I look at his black uniform. I notice his name badge. It has the name William across it, with a gold badge pinned below it. I look to Max; his uniform does not have the same symbol, just his name. I look at both of them, they are both staring at me. Max begins to grow restless.

"Sorry, I do not want to seem ungrateful but…carry me?" I look to the ground slightly embarrassed.

Max laughs unexpectedly catching on to what I had implied.

William rushes in to apologise.

"Sorry, I did not think. Of course, you do not want to be lodged about. I will go and get you a wheelchair, you look tired."

He shoots a quick dagger filled stare towards young Max, which causes him to stand up straighter and completely stop laughing, stopping himself from appearing unprofessional. Satisfied, he turns around and runs back to the metal security door.

"So, Max, what brings you here?"

I nervously try to make idle chit chat with Max. He looks at me clearly amused with my feeble attempt.

"Well, Victoria, I work here," he smirks to himself, pleased with his reply.

Bloody hell, Victoria, could you be any more transparent?

"Of course, sorry, stupid question."

I turn to face the wall, feeling his stare bore into me. Making me feel more and more uncomfortable as the agonising seconds drag by. *Come on, William, hurry up!*

"So, Victoria, how's the leg? I heard you got pretty badly beaten up. It's all any of us can talk about down here," Max makes an attempt to make small talk now, he seems to be doing better than me already.

Shit, is he on to me? Stop it! He's just trying to be nice. If you carry on the way you are, he will catch on to what you are up to. Just try to play it cool, or at least as cool as you can possibly make it.

"Pretty bad to be fair, it is more of an annoyance having to get around on crutches, more than anything."

Well, at least that comment is half true, it is painfully annoying to have to hobble around on crutches, when really you do not actually need them, the freshly healed skin on the palm of my hands do not appreciate me at this moment in time.

Max looks me up and down, he is about to reply when William comes racing up with a wheelchair ready for me.

Thank you, William, you have no idea how much I want to give you a hug right now! I do not know why but being in Max's presence makes me feel increasingly uneasy.

"Here you go, if you would like to take a seat. I will get young Max here to escort you to the head office."

He takes the crutches from me, attaching them to the back of the chair, I awkwardly place myself down, trying my hardest to look like I am in a lot of pain.

Great! Just when I thought William and I could become great friends, He has to go and open his mouth and say that!

Why, William, I thought we were friends? OK, now it looks like I am going to be stuck with Max for longer than I had anticipated. It is OK, I can do this, he isn't that bad. Is he? With that he removes the brakes on the wheelchair and begins to push me towards the door, pushing me with a little more force than needed, making me jolt slightly in the chair, hitting my head on one of the crutches.

"Ouch," I deliberately make a point of letting him know he had caused that pain.

"Sorry, I sometimes forget my own strength," he chuckles to himself.

Something tells me that is a lie. I can imagine Max shows off his strength every chance he gets. He seems to be extremely strong, more so than anyone else I have met. It looks so effortless for him. He does not even have to try. So, I am guessing his primary ability is a strength energy connection. He seems pretty happy about it as well.

I think everyone here at this school has slightly more enhanced strength and are naturally a lot faster and more agile than humans. But it looks like if you specifically have the ability of strength or speed, it is nothing you could possibly imagine. It would make everyone else here look like nothing, and that is saying something, as everyone at this school has enhanced supernatural abilities that are connected and sourced by the kinetic energies that flow through the earth.

Max casually throws out a question, as if we have known each other for a long time.

"Do you have a boyfriend?" Completely caught off guard, I come out of my thoughts unwillingly. I stumble around looking for the right thing to say. *Did he really just ask me that?*

"Um, no, I do not."

My mind instantly goes to Romeo, I know I barely know him, and I am the reason he is in this mess but I cannot explain it. I feel drawn to him. I know it's silly. Hey, he might be seeing someone, that's how little I know about him. It is not like we had talked about if we are mutually exclusive to one another yet, if at all. I wait for an overly confident reply but when I do not get one, I brave a look up towards Max.

He has a massive grin plastered across his whole face. Great, he's clearly happy with my answer. We carry on the rest of the way in silence. William had opened the door for us to go through. I had suspected right. It was a hand scanner as well as an iris identification for security. Once through the thick metal set doors, the tunnel's look completely changes. It is now lined with Red carpets. The walls full of hanging pictures. Countless plaques in remembrance of those who had given up their lives to protect the school's secret and possibly the world. The walls still carry the white through from the other side. But the lights are less daunting, probably because they are not reflecting off of surgically white floor surfaces.

Modern chandeliers hang evenly throughout, creating a formal but homely feel. I take a mental note every time Max turns down another tunnel, trying to remember my way out. I wonder where Logan is right now? Max pulls back on the wheelchair, as we get closer to a set of double doors, these ones, unlike the others, are wooden, maybe oak. It still has a security pad but this one is only a card. Max stops and swipes his security card, then leans his back up against the door, to push his way through but before he does, he stops, to ask one last question.

"If you would like, once you have finished up in there, maybe we could discuss me taking you on a date, you know? If that's cool with you?"

He stands rigid, waiting for my reply, his face looks vulnerable, he looks even younger than he had before.

"Really, Max, you have barely spoken to me, now you want to take me out on a date?"

Frown forms above my eyes, frustrated by the delay.

I just want to get on the other side of these doors, and set everything straight.

"Yeah, I guess I am," he raises a hand and adjusts his collar, trying to show he couldn't care less about what I have to say.

"Sure, whatever you say." I throw out a rushed reply, just wanting to get this over with. I have a feeling if I do not give him the answer he wants to hear, I'll be stuck out here even longer.

Satisfied by my answer, Max pushes through the doors but no one is in the room. He keeps pushing me, until we get to a couch. This must be a waiting room. I look over to the far wall, yes, there looks to be another room behind those doors.

"I will go to let them know you are here."

I watch as he walks away. He presses a buzzer, a woman's voice asks who it is. Max gives a code, clearly meant for extra security and the door opens. After that, I am left alone in the room, suddenly all too aware of what I am to do next. *Shit, what if they tell him that they did not ask for me? What have I done?* But before I can go into full panic mode, Max comes back out with a beautiful, heavyset woman. They both walk back towards where I am placed next to the couch, sat in this wheelchair, with little to no padding. The lady openly welcoming me.

"Hello, Miss Luna-Maddicks, I am so happy you could finally join us."

A knowing look in her eye but she does not seem surprised by my being here. She turns to Max and addresses to him.

"Thank you, Max, you may go back to your position," she gives him a warm motherly smile.

Max looks reluctant to leave; clearly, he had thought he would be staying. But he does not disobey her orders, knowing she is the one in charge in this contemporary room. He steals a quick glance at me, leaving a parting smile but of course, he had to open his mouth and speak.

"I'll see you after," he winks at me, then quickly makes a smooth exit.

Once he is gone, and surely out of hearing range, the woman before me looks over to me, the look on her face now is not as welcoming as it originally had been moments before.

"Miss Luna-Maddicks, what brings you here? I know Max has told me 'we' sent for you. But both you and I know that is not true."

I knew everything had been going way too smoothly, it had to hit the fan eventually.

"I have come here to tell you that it was not Romeo who did this to me. It was the Elders in the cave under the lake. He had only come to save me when he had seen the signal for help I had sent out."

This is the moment I have been waiting for. I need to tell her everything now. So she can stop whatever it is they are doing.

"Is that so? How could you possibly know anything about the elders? For one, there is no cave under the lake. You have only been here a few days. He has clearly messed with your emotions to try and save himself."

She walks over to the table, which has a coffee machine on top and casually helps herself to a cup of coffee, as though this is a typical everyday encounter to her.

"Besides you're too late, he has been sent to the main base in Australia. This school is merely a stopping ground in comparison. You can go now."

She picks up her reusable coffee cup, clearly bored by the whole thing, to walk back the way she had come.

"Wait, what do you mean, I am telling the truth. Where is he? Tell me, I will go there and tell them myself. He is innocent."

I beg for her to understand, to help me.

"You silly girl, no one knows where it is. Only those with the highest authority know. We are not going to go around telling silly little girls like yourself."

Before I have the chance to demand answers, she quickly makes her exit through the doors.

What just happened? Why didn't she believe me?

I stay seated for a little longer, not quite sure how to process what had just happened? It seems as though it did not matter what I had to say, she was never going to believe. My emotions begin to well up. I try desperately to hold them back, why now? I need to stay strong. *Please don't cry,* I try to talk myself down. All I need is for that monster of a woman to walk back through those doors and see me crying. I can picture her cackling with laughter right now if she ever gets to witness the blubbering mess that I have turned into.

OK, I need to find Logan. I go to reach for my crutches, automatically playing the part of still being critically injured but instead of standing up and hobbling my sorry ass out of this place that clearly goes out of their way to crush integrable young minds, I make a quick judgment call. It appears that no one could care less about me or what I have to say. So, I decide to ditch the crutches and walk right on out of here as if a miracle had just taken place in that very room. It would be funny to see the look on the face of whoever reviews the footage being captured right now.

To actually see what they have to say about the video footage of me being wheeled in here in a wheelchair, and hobbling my way into these very tunnels and room, only to turn around and walk out that very same door.

Priceless, also some well-deserved payback. I open the door and walk straight out looking to see which way I should go. Should I stay to do some more digging? See if I can find out some actual helpful Information of Romeo's whereabouts? Because I cannot possibly go to find Logan, only to tell him that I could do nothing in the means of saving his brother. That all I got was that he is at the secret Australian base, which, I quote, 'the location cannot be given out to silly little girls like me'.

ERH, she was so infuriating. I just wanted to scream in her face.

As I walk down the opposite way I came in through, I notice the cosy feel of the tunnels start to change, becoming more profound, and deeper as I travel down them. The red plush carpets are swapped out for dirty grey tiles, the walls a dirty white. Clearly, this part of the tunnels are visited far less than the other headquarters. I walk a little longer but realise if I am to find anything, it won't be down here, I need to go back to where all the action took place and is.

Chapter 12

The tunnels are eerily quiet, *Where is everybody?* I jump a mile when I hear my name break through the ringing dead silence.

"Victoria, Victoria, wait up!"

Logan had come to find me just like he had promised. I hesitate a moment before waiting for him to catch up. I do not turn around, what am I going to say to him? He is going to be so disappointed. He already thought I was dead weight back when I was still injured, maybe he may wish, I still am. He'll probably happily put me back in that hospital bed himself.

"Victoria, are you OK?" The reasoning behind this question is because I am yet to turn and thoroughly look at him, since he has managed to catch up with me. Once I had started walking again in no particular direction, all I know is that I do not want to see the look of utter disappointment, grief-stricken across his face when I have to tell him what happened. The look of despair would be too much, my thoughts deliberately drift over to those of my little sister, reflecting on the possible loss of an individual's loved one, their pending doom, not being fully known, is she still laying in a hospital bed in a coma? I have not heard anything. The doctors had promised to let me know if there was any change in her circumstances.

I still do not reply to Logan's concerned words, lost in my own selfish thoughts. Logan gets the drift of my wandering mind, my unhelpful ideas flowing haphazardly, causing a shift in my persona towards him. He rushes in, to swoop in to comfort me. Not knowing what indeed is on my mind.

"It is OK, I know about Romeo. I got the intel from some guys I was last on a mission with," his voice saddens as it comes to the end of his sentence.

He should be the last person trying to make me feel better. I should be the one to make him feel better. Not the other way round. I look up to him then, sadness manifesting in both our eyes.

"What are we going to do?"

I stop, as there is no real point to us carrying on walking, it is better if we get something planned before we go any further.

"We are going to make a little visit to Australia, I have always wanted to go," he smiles, half-heartedly.

"Australia? But no one knows where the base is located. How are we meant to find it?"

My voice raises an octave higher than I had intended but my point still stands. How the hell is a bunch of young adults, well individuals like us, meant to go to a place that is so well hidden only a select few know where it is located?

All I can imagine is us wandering around Australia like a bunch of headless chickens running around in endless circles. We are genuinely screwed. What are we going to do? I need to figure out these powers of mine before we do anything else. On another note, I really need to give my endless mind babble a revamp, so it starts putting more positive and constructive advice and criticism inside of this mind of mine! First things first, I really need to stop being so hard on myself.

"Good thing I know people. I have contacts that are based all around Australia, they may not be able to tell us where exactly it is but they will be able to get us close enough that we might actually have a chance of finding it. Well, I am hoping."

Logan stands strategically in front of one of the pictures on the wall, looking as though he is attempting to impersonate an art inspector at a gallery. He also then continues pretending to recognise multiple portraits of the soldiers hanging on all the walls. Clearly trying to avert his attention to anything else, as he is not actually paying any real attention to them at all.

"OK, I think before we go anywhere, can we head to the training room? So I can give these abilities of mine a test drive. What do you think?" I wait eagerly for his response.

"I know we don't exactly have a lot of time, as we are on a deadline. One that continues to loom ever so quickly towards Romeo's unknown pending circumstances but I need to at least give it a shot. I have only done a few classes of combat and two that actually required me trying to use my gifts, which at the time had been a waste, as I was yet to tap into them."

Logan looks at me a moment as he thinks this over in his mind, trying to come up with the best option for us. I am so glad I have him here to help, as I am pretty sure, if I had tried to attempt this on my own, I would not have gotten this far. For one, I had no idea about these tunnels we currently stand in that lay beneath the foundations of this school. I definitely do not know anyone here really either. What's that saying? Two heads are better than one.

"Yes, I think that is a good idea, we need all the firepower we can get. But we do not have long, so I will try to jam in all of your training into one quick lesson. It could work but only if you are up to it?"

The energy in the room has changed, the static electricity grows as the adrenaline begins to rise to the surface, shifting the mood.

"I am willing to try anything."

My forehead frowns at the unexpected look on Logan's face.

"What is it?"

I pull out my phone that I had hidden in my moon boot, which I also decide to take off then and there and leave it for someone else to deal with.

"You should really be careful who you say that around, they might just take you up on that."

He chuckles quietly to himself, not fully feeling what he has said. But he said it anyway to try to take some of the severity of the situation out of the tension we both felt.

"Oi, shut it you."

I throw my head back in a forced chuckle, one that is probably a little more forced than actually needed. Now if only I could remember my way out of here.

Logan starts walking in a direction I do not recognise but I do not question it as I have no idea where we are right now, or where we will come out from. We could end up in the toilets for all I know. We walk for quite some time, both lost in our thoughts, thinking over the possibilities of what there is to come? How on earth am I meant to master my abilities in the space of a few hours and how the hell are we going to get to Australia? I do not have any spare cash on me to be able to pay for a flight. I am only 17 for crying out loud, plus I do not have access to the money my parents left behind until I am 18. I still have a while to go yet.

Logan pushes open a hole in the ceiling, then beckons for me to follow. I struggle to climb up to the high ceiling exit, due to the lack of stairs or ladders at hand. I grip to what I can, considering the walls are relatively flat, it is exceptionally challenging to get a proper hold. Logan has a good few inches on me in the height department. Plus, he is just way more trained and experienced than I am. But I do somehow manage to make my way up, not gracefully but I do make it relatively quick, to my surprise.

Well, it may not be the toilets but it is not much better. We have come up through a hidden entrance from the tunnels to the floor that has led us directly to the training room, where all the equipment has been stored in.

The smell of sweat fresh in the air, clearly someone had been here not long ago using this stuff. They clearly did not clean the equipment after they had finished using it. I will be sure to thank them when I find out exactly who it was. I can see why we took the way we did. It has saved us time. Logan had obviously been thinking ahead; also, I am guessing when he said we had to be quick, he meant we are starting straight away. A wave of panic washes over me, *Am I ready for this? I guess we will find out soon enough.*

Logan throws me a skipping rope. I just stand there looking confused, how is this going to help? Logan sees this.

"You need to warm up first, plus it will help me see your fitness level, that way I can plan accordingly."

A little twinkle in his eye plays alongside the smirk he sends my way.

"What do you mean? I am fit and healthy, I used to take part in a lot of sport. I am sure I will be fine."

I walk off to find some space, then start skipping slow at first then faster, trying to bring my heart rate up. I will show him what I am made of.

Logan knocks me sideways by throwing a sand ball at my head, with no fair warning. I slowly try to get up, my head pounding inside my skull.

"What the hell, Logan? You could have at least warned me."

I hold my head in both my hands trying to keep it together, it feels as though it has been cracked down the middle like an egg.

"You are meant to use your powers to block it, I need to see if your abilities are more defensive or attack."

He writes a note down on his mobile phone, making notes of my fractured head no doubt. How was that even fair? How can I defend when I do not know I need to?

"I did it without your knowledge to see if your abilities would manifest and react for you, which they have before. But it must only work when you feel threatened, nice to know you trust me."

He walks away to go find something else to throw at me, no doubt.

"You mean I used to trust you until you fractured my skull," I throw metaphorical daggers at him, if I could throw actual knives at him right now, I would.

I stand up and assess the damage he has so kindly caused me. I notice blood on my hands. Great! I am going to have to heal myself again, I suppose I might as well get the practice in. Last time, I had to feel for the energy and pull it from the earth but I am inside at the moment in a building where there are only skylights for windows, how will I draw my energy from nothing? Then I remember that everything around us has its own unique energy signal, plus I just have to find it.

I crouch down and place my bloodied hand on the floor beneath me, searching for the energy I need, I clear my thoughts and focus on connecting to the energy's direct heat sauce, to draw it close to me. I feel undiluted vibrations entering my fingertips and slowly sending waves up my arms and through my whole body.

Wow! This feels amazing, different from the energy I pulled from the earth but just as powerful. I cannot feel the specific pull of energy I need to heal myself but I do feel something else there. I look up to see where Logan is. I wonder, payback's a bitch.

I raise one of my hands directing it towards Logan, I pull the exact energy frequency that had sent vibrations up through me, and send it to the ends of my fingertips, urging it to hit Logan. A sonic vibration pulsates from my hand and towards where Logan stands with his back to me. It hits him so hard; he flies through the air hitting the back wall. Shit, I didn't mean for that much energy to flow through me. I run over to him to see if he is OK. But before I get to him, he is already getting up and ready to stand back up on his own feet.

"I am so sorry; I did not think it would be that powerful." I look him up and down checking for any damage, he appears to be OK.

"That was unexpected but, wow, that was amazing. How did you do that? I felt the vibration push through my very being creating a blast that sent me flying, only it wasn't a force. It was more the rate of the vibrations traveling through me were so great it caused me to vibrate across the room, that is insane."

OK, that was not what I was expecting at all. He looks to me then with a whole new look of admiration and respect.

"You, Miss Victoria Luna-Maddicks, are a force to be reckoned with, you are truly unique. That kind of power you sent out, with little to no training, is just unheard of," he looks at me a while longer with a question in his eyes.

"Let's see what else you can do? Try touching something else, and see what ability it will give you."

He looks like a kid that has been told he can have anything he wants from the candy store.

I walk over to the wall closest to me, again placing my palm against it to feel and draw the energy towards me. Once I pick it up, I welcome it to connect with. This time, the power feels almost stiff, slow to come to the surface. I let it take its time while it charges itself up. When I feel as though enough energy has gathered, I direct my hand, this time away from Logan. I call for it to come to the surface, as it passes through me, I can feel as it leaves my fingertips, I wait to see what it will do. When I see nothing, I look over to Logan to ask him if I had just been lucky with it the first time but when I do, I notice Logan standing perfectly still, in the same position as he had been in, still waiting patiently to see what happens only he does not move at all, almost as though he is frozen in time. *Wow.* I walk over and wave my hand in front of the fixed expression on his good-looking face. Still nothing.

I wonder If I can again channel and feel the sluggish energy in me, even though I am no longer touching the wall, will it still work? I send the energy out again, to my surprise it works. Logan blinks, and his chest falls and rises again. Looking thankfully alive and well, he looks to me to see if I have done anything yet when he sees me standing right next to him, when moments ago, I had been standing by the wall, confusion as clear as day on his face.

"What's wrong, are you OK? Maybe you have to wait a little longer for it to work?"

Logan pats me on the shoulder to reassure me but what he does not know yet is that it did work.

"Logan, you were frozen still. You were not moving; you were not even breathing!"

I look to him, waiting for him to go running for the hills, I am waiting for him to run away in fear, what could he possibly think of me?

"That is all out of this world crazy. OK, let's try something else."

He starts walking over to the equipment at hand, he looks back when he notices I have not followed suit.

"You are OK with all this, are you not scared?"

I turn away not wanting to see his realisation of how he actually feels about all of this.

"What? no way. You, Miss Luna-Maddicks, are amazing. I could only dream of the things you have achieved in this short time of knowing everything you know. I do not fear you; I admire you," he walks back over to me and gives me a hug; his masculine muscles are surprisingly comfortable. Considering how firm they are, I allow myself to relish in them a moment longer.

Chapter 13

OK, I think I have everything, my bags are packed. I had asked Logan if he was doubly sure we do not need our passports but he had repeatedly reassured me that we do not, as we are not actually going to be going through the standard customs you would usually be required to. He had asked a few favours to get us a private jet, a government one at that. We are now walking up the stairs to get ready to take off for Australia. I am still only starting to fully grasp the concept of what sort of military machinery and resources we appear to have at our disposal, it seems we are the government's secret weapon when it comes to firepower.

"Not long now," Logan leans over and opens the blind to the plane window. As he pulls away to take his seat he slows down and stares into my eyes.

"Are you ready for this?" I feel his warm breath against my flushed face.

"Yes, I am ready."

I look away before my face burns a brilliant red giving me away. I stare out onto the asphalt taking in the surrounding area. I watch as the team below do the last bits for taking off. I watch as they top up the plane with fuel to carry us to our required destination.

"So where are we heading exactly?"

The twitch to my eye regrettably seems to be getting the better of me, as my nerves batter around ruthlessly within the confinements inside of me, with no sign of surrendering anytime soon. The nervous twitch is my anxiety's way of trying to climb out to the surface, so it can be known to the world. I continue to fight it, not wanting to show Logan how frightened I really am. I tend to blink a bit too frequently when

I am nervous; weird, I know, but it is just one of my little quirks.

"We are going to be flying into Sydney, I am hoping we will have the chance to talk to a few people there. I have been told they are waiting for our arrival, and they will help us out with anything they know."

Logan sits in his seat looking over to me, while eating some peanuts, throwing another one into his mouth while he takes a break from talking.

"OK, so is it based in Sydney then?" I reach over and pinch one of his peanuts, slowly placing it into my mouth, waiting patiently for his reply.

"No, I don't think it is. That would be too obvious but we need to go there to start with, to see what we can find out."

I look over to ask him for another one of his peanuts but Logan has decided at that moment to pull out his complimentary luxury satin sleeping mask. Placing it over his flawless sun-kissed skin, securing it correctly to ensure no sunlight comes through, he has settled down for the journey ahead. I suppose I should do the same thing.

I roll over intending to fall asleep but I can do everything else but that. My mind will just not switch off, going through all the possible outcomes that could happen. What if I cannot draw the energy from around me? What if I turn out to be wholly useless and cause more harm than good? I need to stop this; how can I switch off this whirlwind of chaotic emotions that keep firing off inside my head? I seem to be really good at this whole self-deprecating thing nowadays.

I pull the headphones out of the packaging and place them over my ears. I then press play on the movie I have selected. I watch for a few seconds, confused as to why there is no sound, I turn the volume up. Still nothing? Maybe it has been muted, I look through the settings, nope it is not muted. I then look at the connection of the headphone. Of course, it would help if I actually plugged them in, in the first place for them to actually work! Seriously? I think my nerves are getting the best of me, how am I going to do this? I cannot even use headphones correctly, let alone save Romeo.

I couldn't even save my parents. A single tear rolls down my cheek, I wipe it away before it has a chance to be seen. It still pains me every time I think of them. Will it ever get easier?

The pilot announces over the speaker that we are preparing for landing. Wow! That went fast. I guess that is what happens when you are deep in thought. I had not even noticed the world around me shift, and change.

As we begin to descend through the yellowing atmosphere, landing with the sun as it is getting ready to set in the last of the day's remaining sky, preparing itself for the night ahead.

I stare out over the horizon as I tiptoe behind Logan. He is greeted by two men in uniform. I don't really feel up for talking, so I walk over to continue staring at the extravagant variety of colours colliding together to make the perfect sunset before me. Oranges and reds merge with each other, creating a perfectly balanced shade of perfection, even little hints of purple surface through, joining the pink hues of the setting sun. I look towards it, letting it soothe my nerves. Maybe, I should use the sun's energy to power up, I know I cannot physically touch the sun but I can feel the heat of the sun rays against my soft skin. Maybe that is all I need, to draw in its unique signature energy force. Why not? If you do not try, you will never find out. I close my eyes as I feel the heat of the rays against the surface of my skin, warming the longer I stand there. I focus my thoughts and try to project my energy out to reach for the sun, to help them become entwined and as one. I push it so hard but before it has a chance to fully connect it snaps back into me. Great! That went according to my plan. Not! Now I just feel exhausted, I take a deep breath to steady myself. OK, I will try one more time. I do not want to leave myself depleted. I won't be any good to anyone then.

This time I decide to ease into it, not to force too much, or to push it too hard.

I just let it feel its way to the sun's unique energy force, once it senses a strong point in the energy barrier, it hooks itself onto the electrical current. But I stay still, not forcing my energy to connect with it, I let the sun's energy make the decision to fully join us. I do not want to push myself onto its personal life force that would not be kind. I need to show the sun that I respect it, and that I will not force it to do anything it doesn't want to do. That way when we do connect, the connection is in its purest form. One cannot work fully together if there is no mutual respect between one another. If the link is trusted, then it will not be lost. If I ever need to connect with it again, it will be welcomed. Not rejected in fear.

I feel a sharp tug, then all of a sudden, a rush of fiery energy courses through my veins. *Wow.* I send a meaningful thank you into the connection of the fully formed energy force between me and the blasting heat wave of the sun's energy.

I welcome it wholeheartedly, letting it energise me. I guess I am never going to need to drink coffee again. This is better than any amount of caffeine in the world. I feel beyond magnificent. I smile to myself, letting it fill me to the brim from the inside out, feeling complete joy and wholeness in that very moment. This energy does not feel foreign to me, I ponder over this thought for a moment. Then it hits me, I have already connected with the sun before, only now I did it intentionally. The last time I had done so, it had been an accident, one that had caused my friend's life to be taken away from her. Leaving the forest floors and trees around me charred and scorched to the ground. But this time, it feels different. I feel more connected, I have more control over it.

I draw in as much of the sun's unique and potent energy force that is possible for me to contain inside of my own energy vessel, then I let the connection break, as the sun prepares to disappear, going faster now I have let it go. I decide to see what Logan and the two gentlemen have been talking about. I walk over to them; still deep in conversation, they do not notice me at first. My name passes through Logan's slender lips.

"I cannot ask Victoria to do that."

He rushes to my defence. What could I possibly not want to do?

One of the guys, the shorter one, replies,

"Well, if I could, I would send you but they want a girl, not a boy. Sorry but this is the only way you will be able to get answers."

He looks over to me, noticing me walking over to them. "Why don't we ask her if she is willing to do it?"

The taller broader guy looks at me with a hunger in his eyes.

"Ask me to do what?" I look at the two gentlemen, then to Logan.

The shorter guy looks at Logan, Logan shoots him a disapproving look. He carries on anyway.

"We need you to go undercover as a stripper to get important information, from the manager who owns Bondi Basement."

The hunger in his eyes intensifies as he pictures me, on a stripper pole no doubt.

"Why would this manager have any information in the first place?"

I look disgustedly at the man before me, who does he think he is?

"He used to work at the Australian base within the government's highest-ranked soldiers, as a protector. But he got fired due to reasons we cannot share with you."

Just as I think the shorter guy is about to continue to share the same pervy persona, taking over from his friend's place but he is quick to change my mind of him, as not wanting to offend me any further, he gives the taller broader male a jab to the side to warn him.

"So, you want me to go there and pretend to be a stripper to get intel but you won't tell me what it was he did to get fired? How does that work?"

A frown forms over my facial expressions, leaving distinct indents on my skin.

"Victoria, you do not have to do this."

Logan comes swooping in to my rescue, he seems to be making a habit of this. Not that I am complaining. At the moment, that is.

"Well, is this the only option we have to get the coordinates to find the location of where they are keeping Romeo?"

I look to him for his reply, one that I hoped would tell me there is. But instead of coming up with a better plan, he simply looks away from me, defeat clearly written across his facial features.

"I will take that as a yes."

I take a deep breath and sigh into the beginnings of the night sky, one that I am yet to know what it will bring. Me, a stripper?

We are directed over to a stretch jet black hummer; well this is one way to get noticed, which completely defeats the whole idea of going incognito.

"I know you think this is a sure way to get us noticed but they believe if you hide in plain sight, then you are less inconspicuous, here's hoping anyway."

Logan places his arm over my shoulder once we are seated, keeping a protective stance over me, to frankly warn the other two men away. I look at all the lights scattered perfectly throughout the hummer, with a star-like appearance, accentuating the lights carefully placed through the ceiling. It has an overall dark ambiance to it, with neon lights to add that nightclub feel to it. There is a bar next to where Logan and I have seated ourselves with an array of different variety of alcoholic beverages. An ice bucket to one side, with a silver scoop, to remove the ice cubes into a glass, one that is being used right now. A golden-brown liquid leaves its vintage 1987 bottle, the taller guy swirls the fluid around his glass, sniffing it before taking a savoury sip.

"I love good whiskey."

I lay my head against Logan's shoulder, taking comfort in its familiar warmth and security. I breathe in the smell that lingers on his jacket. It is his own unique individual scent, with an ever so slight hint of a woody scented aftershave. I close my eyes for a moment, letting this feeling wash over me, Logan makes me feel so safe and protected. I do not know what I would do without him here. Our friendship has grown in tremendous leaps and bounds since we first met. I know I can trust him; he knows he can trust me too.

I open my eyes to the sound of someone deliberately clearing their throat to get everyone's attention.

"So, Victoria, we have some wigs and outfits for you to choose from. We will be dropping you off at the main entrance. That is where you will be let in. We have already arranged for your name to be on the list, they will know you as Lexi Smith. You will go through and head over to the furthest part of the basement, go past the bar and to the far door. You will be called in when it is your turn to audition. There is normally two guys in there who watch but we will create a disturbance to get one of the men out; the manager's right-hand guy. That way, you will have him to yourself to get the answers you need. Is there anything else you need me to go over again before you get ready?"

He pulls out one of the selected outfits that I am apparently meant to be wearing from its sleeve. Well, there does not seem to be much material to cover anything really in this particular outfit he has picked out for me.

"Yes, how long do I have till I have to go in?" I bite my bottom lip waiting in anticipation.

"You have about fifty minutes before we get you ready, and this hummer pulls up outside of 'The Bondi Basement'." Next, he pulls out a pair of vibrant red stilettos, with transparent heels.

"Is this a good time to mention that I have never stripped before, and I sure as hell have no idea how to work a pole?"

I fidget with the six-inch heels he has just passed to me to try on.

"You will be fine, watch the other girls who will be inside already performing, just copy what they do, and try to seduce the manager into giving you the answer you need," he winks at me, making me feel uncomfortable in my own skin, which makes me realise the severity of the situation and what I am about to actually do. Here goes nothing.

Chapter 14

Damn, I look good. I look absolutely mesmerising. Even I would fall victim to my sexual appeal right now. Not that I think women should be sexualised in any way just to please a man, but I have to admit I feel good. I feel sexy and empowered within my own body confidence. I can do this.

I went for the six-inch, velvet black, knee-high boots, followed through with the jaw-dropping black short shorts made of leather, with a black lace bra, with red ribbon woven skilfully throughout. The detail is so divine; apparently, this is handmade, especially for this occasion, when did I get so lucky? Of course, I asked if I could keep it after this whole ordeal. Guess what? They said, yes.

It has almost made this occasion, where I have to pretend to be a stripper thing, that bit more worthwhile except the apparent reason being Logan, I mean Romeo. *Oops. Victoria, you are doing this for Romeo, remember? Do not forget why you are here in the first place, OK?* I make a mental note to maybe keep my distance from Logan, after all, he is Romeo's brother. That would not look good in my books. My moral compass would be spiking off the charts if I ever allowed myself to stoop to such levels. One cannot merely inflict such pain on an individual. Life is hard enough without any extra added complications to one's mental health.

The hummer has pulled up outside of the 'Bondi Basement', where I am to make my way up to the main entrance, which has a display of neon lights, blasting the name of the club to everyone who passes by. I personally think they are slightly on the tacky side but it is up to the individuals' taste, which in this case is not mine. As I walk along the red carpet laid out between the matching red ropes, which I have only ever seen when going to the theatre up London. I slowly descend to where I need to be, stopping to be checked in through the list; the very list they had just been telling me about back in the hummer, the very same one that has just pulled around the corner out of sight. I know this because it was part of the plan, they made me go over, again and again, to make sure I knew what it was.

The very list kept by the security woman standing right in front of me now, guarding the main entrance. As I deliberately approach the muscular but slender woman, my heart skips an intentional beat, *This is it.* The woman asks for my name, which I give to her.

"Lexi Smith."

I give one last look behind me, just for reassurance, looking for nothing in particular.

But nonetheless, it helped ease some of my aggressively growing nerves. She looks me up and down, then pulls her radio up to her slim-lined lips, as she says each word. It plays out in slow motion before me, as she calls my name over the radio attached to her earpiece. She looks to me again, mistaking me watching her every move as a question to why she had not just used the earpiece.

"It broke about half an hour ago. I sent for a replacement but if you want anything done around here, do not ask the people around here. You will have to do it yourself. Hey, if you want a job done properly, do it yourself. Am I right?"

She gives me that private smile like we have been buddies for years. In reality, I have known her for less than mere minutes. We are but strangers to each other. All friends start out as such, right? I return the smile not wanting to speak, afraid I may say too much or sound like I am up to something other than the purpose I am supposedly here for.

"Tom, let the guys inside know I am sending Miss Smith in, make sure one of them directs this woman to the correct place, she will need to be guided to the audition room."

She nods to the guy, who I assume is Tom, as he walks into view, then at me, before pulling back the red robe with a golden hook at each end; only one needed to be removed for me to gain entry.

"May I?" the guy, who is named Tom, had been standing to the side of the corridor, leading down to the basement. He had been hidden in the shadows cast by the array of lights littering themselves all over the place chaotically.

"Yes, you may," I try to give him my best flirtatious smile, using my eyes to draw him in.

He smiles pleasingly back to me and takes hold of my arm, guiding me down the dark corridor. I am only able to see every now and then where I am walking due to the dancing lights making themselves known, now and then, adding to the ever-growing atmosphere of the club…

"Wait here, till your name is called."

Before he completely turns away from me, to walk back from the way we had both just come, he gives me a quick wink followed by,

"Good luck in there."

He gives me one last smile, and a slight squeeze of my bare-skinned arm, which has an excessive amount of body glitter sprayed onto it if you ask me. Logan wanted more. He said I have to look believable if I want to pull this thing off.

After the whole flirtatious exchange between the two of us, Tom casually walks away.

OK, that is not what I expected. He was so unexpectedly lovely. The way the others were talking about this place, they led me to believe this place was full of assholes. He quite clearly is not, and I will tell you, the view as he casually made his way back up the way we had come from. I am not complaining; he has one beautiful piece. A hot package at the back there, right there in my line of vision now. The way his back curves leaving his ass to stand out that much more. It protrudes in all the right ways, I bite my plump painted red lips, trying to control myself momentarily.

I am sure he would do well for himself here as a stripper if it does not work out for him as a tour guide. He could quite literally guide me anywhere he likes, preferably to my bedroom. OK, I am joking. I would never subject an individual in that way, turning them into some sex object, degrading the individual in such a way it makes them feel like nothing more than a piece of meat that needs to be tenderised.

Plus, the way I just described myself letting him guide me anywhere he pleases sends out a very poor message. Come on, it would be me leading him, no one can tell me what I want to do with my body. If I want it, I will be more than happy to take part but I am not one to be led. I will be the one calling the smouldering hotshots, so much so they will have to call the fire brigade to put out the flames in this place, and that will be when the real fun starts.

But always remember it is your body, your rules. Never let anyone tell you any different. No, means No. Even when a yes turns to a no, it is now a no. Not an 'I will pressure you till you feel the need to turn it back to a yes'.

I wait nervously by the back of the club, slightly to the left. I watch as each exotic dancer takes to the stage showing off their talent and skills. I try to take as many mental notes as possible as I wait for my name to be called, well, my stripper name to be called. I try the title out inside of my head: *Lexi Smith, would you please take to the stage and show us your stuff?*

Who am I kidding? I am so not going to be able to do any of that, they have months, years even of training. How can I expect myself to just go up to the pole and fake it? I hopefully make it when it takes a lot of hard work and training to master the skill of pole-dancing.

I need to come up with another plan and quick. I bite at the skin on the very edge of my nails, over and over again, my anxiety going through the roof. As I try to stimulate another plan that I can actually pull off successfully, just when I think all hope is lost, a simple but achievable plan comes to mind.

I know. I will just try to talk to him, ask him for the information he has that I need, maybe use slight persuasion. Worst case scenario, I will have to kindly give him an ultimatum. I am still thankfully charged up from the energy of the sun earlier. I have had no reason to use it. Yet, I can use that as a last resort. You know, if he does not give me what I need, I'll just burn the place down to the ground. I will explain to him; it is as simple as that.

"Lexi Smith?"

A tall, balding man appears in the archway of the door, leading into the audition room I have been waiting outside for the last twenty minutes. He looks me up and down.

"Well, are you Lexi?" he asks the question in a frustrated manner, not wanting to waste any more time than he has to.

"Yes, that is me."

Well, for tonight it is. I walk over to him. He moves out of the way to let me squeeze past him to get into position. As I walk in, the first thing I notice is the pole in the middle of the room. It is gold and, of course, reaches from the floor to the ceiling. I gulp as I look it up and down, walking up to it makes it look no less daunting. Its appearance makes my very being want to just seize up right there and then. *Get it together, Victoria, I mean, Lexi. Here goes nothing.*

The balding man walks over to his seat. Once seated, he watches as I stand there in front of him, waiting for me to begin my performance. But unfortunately for him, that will not be happening tonight. I go to speak, to ask if I can ask him a question, when another man walks deliberately and purposefully through the door. The wind that had been created through the action of the door being thrown open in what would be called an over dramatic entrance, now, accumulates together to create a pocket that burst as he passes by me, from his body creating a force with the speed he walks with. OK, great! I did not anticipate there being two men, this is going to be tricky. I had thought the guys had said they were taking care of that.

I grab onto the pole to appear as though I am about to start my performance. I do not know why I bothered as I look up. I notice the two men deep in conversation. I playfully swing around the pole, just getting a feel for what it would actually be like to use one, not that I am. But curiosity calls. I continue to fool around with the pole waiting for the men to pay attention, forgetting they may actually be watching. I lift a leg on to the cold, metal cylinder shape to see if I could pull off one of the moves the dancers were doing outside on stage but just as I had thought, I terribly and drastically fail. I clearly do not know what I am doing. I manage to spin wildly out of control, getting my legs tangled up in the process. Smashing shamelessly into the ground. *Ouch.*

I pull myself up begrudgingly, almost falling again as I lose my balance in these ridiculous heels. I straighten out my barely-there clothing, pulling my knee-high boots back up to my knees. I look up, to my dismay the two men had been watching, they had been watching the whole damn thing. *Shit, this is not good. OK, think. Play it cool. Act as though you were just warming up.*

I smile and go to place my hand back onto the pole to pose in my alluring stance, well, that was the plan anyway but I miss entirely, completely misjudging where my hand had needed to fall; resulting in misjudging where the pole had been initially, not that it had moved. But there is no need to get into the semantics, which results with me miserably falling flat on to the levelled floor that continues to involuntarily quicken to my ever-nearing face, to my fall to the ground. I even slide along the floor for a second from the sheer force of my body weight hitting the waxed floorboards. Loud, ear-piercing thud echoes unmistakably through the room. I roll over on the floor, momentarily winded from the whole ordeal. I look up to the ceiling. But as I do, I notice the balding man standing over the chaos that is me all over the floor, not looking impressed in the slightest.

"You are not here to audition, are you?"

The man asks it more as a statement than a question but I use this to my advantage. I jump up more gracefully than the whole display I had just given him, throwing him off balance.

"Great observation but there is something you can do for me."

I fling my hair out of my face, trying to look as presentable as possible, and as together as I can, especially after that little disaster they had just witnessed first-hand.

"Really now, what may that be?" he looks me up and down, looking slightly amused and interested in what I could possibly have to say.

Here goes nothing.

"I need you to give me the location of the Australian school base?"

I look on hopefully, hoping it will be this easy.

"Assuming I know what you are talking about," he looks back over to the guy behind him, quickly signalling for him to leave the room. He does so without question. *Shit.*

"Why would I tell you? What benefit does it have to me?" he raises his eyebrows, waiting for my answer.

"Good point."

I think this over for a second, not wanting to prolong the situation, giving him the upper hand.

"Well, if you tell me, I will leave your club in one piece. If you don't, well, I guess you will find out."

I look him dead in the eye, not breaking eye contact. He does the same, not appearing intimidated in the slightest.

"You? What could you possibly do?"

He throws his head back in laughter. OK, this is not how I saw this turning out.

OK, here goes nothing. I draw the energy source from earlier to the surface, trying to centre it directly to the palm of my hand. I welcome it like the morning sun, soaking up its warmth. Not wanting to actually, accidentally set this whole place on fire, well yet. As I feel the palm of my hand beginning to heat up. I know I have managed to control the energy well enough that I feel confident I can release it.

A burst of flames radiate from my hands, making the balding man stand back.

They settle down, just becoming ignited blue balls of fire in the delicate, unharmed palms of my hands. I smile, pleased with my efforts. The look on his face says it all. It was not what he had been expecting here tonight.

"Even if I knew where it was, I cannot tell you. I have been sworn by secrecy. If they find out I was the one to tell you, trust me, it would not end well for either of us. Why do you want to know, anyway?"

He keeps a careful eye on my hands, waiting for the moment I change my mind and plan on attacking him, which I will, unless I have no other choice. But he does not know that.

"I am looking for a friend, they took him to the base here in Australia."

I move my arms around to show him I mean here in Australia, not that I needed to but I always seem to talk with my hands, trying to get the point across.

"He was taken under false pretences. I need to get there so I can clear his name. Will you help me?"

My eyes fill with a surge of need, I try to stop it but the need is too much, I cannot hide it anymore.

"What is his name?"

He walks over to his desk, looking for something amongst the organised chaotic mess.

"Romeo, his name is Romeo."

I try to think of what his last name could be, I should have asked Logan. How can I not know it? The flames in my hand begin to flicker and spat. The man at the desk takes note of this, noticing my lack of control over my emotions.

"Romeo, I think I have heard that name floating around people's conversation in the last few days. Something about him brutally trying to kill a young woman down by the sacred Elders' lake."

He stops then looking me over again, this time with a knowing stare.

"Are you that girl he supposedly tried to kill, is that why you are here?"

He is quick to put the two together, not much gets past him by the looks of it.

"Yes, that girl was me. As you can see, I am fine now. It was not him who had harmed me, it had been the Elders themselves."

I rush to explain, wanting to tell the truth to whoever would listen. Hoping it would somehow get back to those who held him.

"The Elders? They were the ones to harm you?" he walks out from behind his desk, now pacing up and down the audition room that doubles as his office, thinking over this new piece of information I have just given him.

"I am assuming this is what he had told them when they questioned him about what had happened."

His face puzzles over, trying to make sense of this all. Then all of a sudden, the realisation dawns upon him.

"If this is true, and the Elders were the ones to harm you, and this friend of yours told the leaders this; it makes sense why they rushed him off so quickly. I am assuming you already tried to explain this to them and they did not want to hear a word of it, correct me if I am wrong."

He stops to stare at me, when I say nothing with the look plastered across my face, absolutely speechless. He continues on.

"If I am correct in assuming, I know what they are thinking. Which I should be. I worked there for many, many years. Your friend is being framed. Due to them not wanting anyone to find out what the Elders are capable of. In fear of losing respect and control over all their people."

He pulls out his phone and sends a text message quicker than I have the chance to stop him.

"What do you mean? Why would it be so bad if the truth was to be told?"

The flames in my hands grow with the intensity of my ever-increasing emotions, realising the severity of this situation more and more as it all begins to sink in, with the pieces slowly clicking into place, making more sense, with each one securely clicking into its place. *Oh no, Romeo really is in trouble.*

"You see, they have used the Elders for generations to keep the people in line, making sure they all knew who had a direct connection to the Elders, meaning who had control and should be the leader. If they have attacked and harmed one of their own, meaning you…"

He uses his index finger to point towards me, to fully get his point across. As he turns around to reach for something in one of his desks draws, he quickly opens it with the small key he had placed deliberately in his left trouser pocket. Moving too fast for me to keep up with each and every one of his carefully coordinated moves.

"It will show no one actually has any power over the Elders, and that the Elders act on their own rules and their own terms. This shows the weakness of those who lead today. That it is fair game to whoever dares to step forward."

He looks to me then, to see if I am following in what he is trying to get across to me but I am not sure if I am. I think he notices this for himself. Not a moment too late, he seems more than happy to jump in and explain at length what this means for my dear friend Romeo.

"You see, my love, your friend cannot be allowed to tell his story because if he does, all hell will break loose. They are not going to let him go. For one, they need someone they can pin all this insanity on. It seems distraction is their key plan on making this all go away. Secondly, they cannot risk having him alive; if anyone was to find out the truth, well… I think I have told you enough now for you to realise that there is no saving your friend."

Whatever he had grabbed out of his draw now takes priority over what we have been talking about. I stand still where I stood, listening to the God-awful news just a few minutes longer, not sure what to make of this dreadful turn of events. I knew I had to save him. I just was not sure what I was saving him from, until now.

Chapter 15

Why has this have to happen to me now? Of all the times it could come to me, it had to be in the middle of getting what I need from this guy. I know they had said they would help guide me, but this? And so ill-timed. Could they have not checked before sending me crashing down to my knees? In the middle of a brothel? Maybe that is why they did it. Perhaps they do not want me to get the answers I need. I had managed to get the most part from him but I am still yet to get what I had originally come for, and that is the location of the school.

But to my astonishing luck, I have been gifted with what appears to be a vision. I have only personally ever had one other before nor have I ever known someone to be blessed with such visions. Did I say blessed? I mean, cursed. My head falls into the palms of my sweaty hands but they are not made moist from the flame I held in them but from the sheer pain that now rips its way freely through my mind, crumbling me to the floor I had picked myself off moments before, completely distinguishing my light and flame. Leaving me utterly defenceless. In the wake of this strange man. Who knows what he may do to me?

The vision has been sent from the Elders themselves, to help make it easier for me to choose my path. This is conveniently the second time this has happened to me now.

It begins hazy at first, like trying to drive through a thick fog along the motorway. Everyone else still driving like maniacs, not slowing for a second, like there is nothing to navigate through, when really no one could possibly see further than five foot in front of them; the headlights of oncoming cars from the other side of the motorway are barely visible to the naked eye. Only a very compact dimness is seen from the lights, as they navigate their way through, tirelessly trying to break their way through the stagnant fog. But like all fog, it begins to lift and fade, leaving behind a perfectly clear image before me, allowing me to finally see what had been waiting on the other side all this time. I slowly start to be able to make out an image of me standing on a white sandy beach. The sand is so fine, every time I take a step it squeaks, holding me to where I stand. I bend down to pick up a handful of this divine silk-like sand, letting it slide through my delicate fingers, one grain at a time.

I hear a squeal from a distance. I look up to see what this musical sound to my ears could possibly be? What I see next leaves me kneeling in the white marble sand. While I stare in deranged astonishment at what I see right now, my mouth gaping like a tunnel waiting for a train that never comes, my voice has been executed from my body. All that is left behind is a hole for where my mouth hangs open.

The young girl, she could not be more than one, waddles towards me, holding onto a teddy bear covered in the white sand that could resemble magical dust. It glimmers in the sunlight, adding to the purity of this young infant child, who in my eyes looks angelic. She reminds me of someone I know. I start to notice the similarities between the two of us. She has my eyes and lips. The same ones I have seen a thousand times in the mirror looking straight back at me.

But she also reminds me of another, that someone else shares her angelic perfection. My eyes so rare and unseen are now reflected in these young infant's eyes as I gaze into them. Confused about how they could possibly be encased in this unearthly, beautiful child's face. She runs straight into my arms as if it were the most natural thing to her in the whole world. I hold onto her for a little while longer, not wanting to let this feeling of pure joy and fulfilment to ever leave me. My heart feels complete, like a piece of the puzzle has only just been found, after a lifetime of searching for it without actually knowing what 'it' was until this very moment.

My eyes begin to well up from the tears that had started gathering the moment I laid eyes on her. The squeal of excitement leaves her lips again as I lift her up and twirl her around, not knowing how I knew this was one of her favourite things to do. My heart beats for her. My soul brightens for her happiness. At this moment, I know that the only thing that truly matters to me is making this little girl happy and making sure she has everything she could ever possibly need and more.

I collapse to the ground, exhausted from the force I have been brutally dragged through inside my mind, pulling and twisting at every chance. If I had ever experienced a hangover before, this is what I would imagine it to feel like but by ten folds. I wait for the room to stop spinning, holding back the vomit that is inching its way up, trying to escape. I focus my eyes onto the pair of tanned dress shoes which are perfectly in line in front of my face, trying to gain all my senses again. I sit back then, lift my head up. The guy I had been speaking to stands over me. I feel so small all the way down here like he could step on me like a bug, and that would be the end of the life I have known and grown to love.

Victoria, stop being so dramatic and get a hold of yourself already.

"Does that happen to you a lot, then?"

He extends his hand out to offer me a hand up. I take it eagerly. Not wanting to prolong this embarrassing moment the Elders have so kindly plagued me with.

"No actually, that is a first."

I lie, knowing full well that this has happened to me once before. I hold the back of my neck with my left hand. I slowly start to massage it, working the kinks out that had knotted up from the whiplash I had just experienced. I really hope that is the last time it happens. I shake my legs out, getting rid of the pins and needles forming in the base of them. Now all I have to do is get through them becoming numb and hope that nothing tries to kill me in the meantime. I make the most of not being able to move, taking this chance to ask and press for more answers to my questions. I notice a shift in his stance. He must have seen mine too. Preparing himself just as I am.

"Can you tell me the location of where Romeo is being held unjustifiably. I need to get him out now!"

I close my eyes, still trying to make the room completely stop spinning. It's more of a wave now than a thunderous rollercoaster, like it had been moments before.

He paces for a brief moment, then turns and looks me directly in the eye; what he says next surprises me beyond belief.

"I am so sorry but I cannot get the words past my lips. If I could, I would tell you right away. I, more than anyone, want to watch the leaders as they fall not so gracefully from their high horse, while they desperately try and crawl their way out of this one, without the help of your unfortunate young friend's life."

Tears well up in his eyes, a vein pulsates in his neck and forehead, he looks like he is about to explode. Maybe he just really needs me to understand him?

"What do you mean? Can you not physically speak the words, or are you too afraid to say them aloud?"

I catch myself staring at the vein on his forehead as it becomes enlarged, more so by the second. It is like it has its own life force coexisting within him as a passenger. One that was not invited.

"I have had my brain manipulated, that makes it impossible for me to ever relay or speak of the location of the school. It is a nifty ability, one that only takes seconds to completely alter the way someone thinks or feels towards things."

He reaches for his suit jacket on the back of his leather chair, studded with silver studs along with the seams. It isn't unusually cold weather outside but he is only wearing a light plain white t-shirt. He catches me staring, so he continues where he had left off before becoming side-tracked with putting on his grey suit jacket, a perfect balance between casual wear and formal attire.

"One switch of a specific neuron impulse in the frontal lobe and it can completely alter an individual's personality. Though it may be quick, it is extremely powerful, and one wrong move could leave the individual brain dead. It is an extremely rare energy absorption. One that can only be accessed by the ability to draw energy from one's own hemispheres of each half of the full brain's chemistry system. You have to be able to navigate your own neuron and cognitive pathways before being able to draw and find your way through someone else's mind."

He picks a wooden toothed comb off his desk with the letters G.O.L.D. engraved into the wooden surface. He quickly but smoothly runs it through his thick jet-black hair, which already has a fine layer of wax or some sort of oil running through his curly mane. He is clearly getting ready to leave, to where I have no idea but I hope whatever he is planning, it involves helping me get the answers I need. He wilfully shoots off a text message to several different people. Maybe, it is only the one individual who knows. All I know is that he is swift but prompt. Clearly, his nimble expeditious hands understand what he's doing. His thumbs moving with a purpose, one that needs to be carried out as fleetingly as possible.

He looks towards me, as if I should already know what is going on right now. I look at him with an evident puzzled expression across my bemused face. I batter my eyelids rapidly, attempting to refocus my attention to see what it is I have evidently missed in the process of the upcoming scene playing out in front of me right now. I stutter for a brief moment; my words are failing me.

"Are you coming?"

He raises his eyebrows in frustration, with his arm outstretched in the direction of the door I had come through previously when I had arrived.

"Ready for what?"

I ask him ambiguously, uncertain of the course of events that led us to this very moment, what had I missed? Did we discuss what was happening now? Am I still recovering from the vision the Elders sent me? I await his sluggish reply, not sure why he is hesitant to do so.

"We just discussed that I have a friend of a friend who can reach into my mind and see what it is I am unable to recall. But to do this, we need to leave now and head over to the gold coast where I last heard she was staying. Are you up for this?" Concern drenches his facial features making him look older than he is.

"Yes, of course, sorry, I just got slightly side-tracked it seems."

Of course, I have no memory of this conversation ever been had, when was this? Maybe it was when I had the vision. I apparently had a full-blown conversation while seeing my future daughter, if I was to follow that path. It seemed like a good one; I do not know why I would not want to pursue such a future. But I am starting to get the feeling that the other visions that will be sent my way won't be so blissfully sweet.

Content with my reply, he does not waste a moment longer. He hurriedly rushes me out the door, and back up the dimly lit corridor leading us back up towards the street, where the entrance to The Bondi Basement stands.

I look around energetically to see if I can see the stretch hummer that had brought me here. I walk further down the road I had previously seen them drive down, as I had stood to wait to be checked in to The Bondi Basement. A deep frown merges across my face. *They said they would be here. Where are they? What if I was actually in some serious trouble right now? I would be completely and utterly screwed. I am going to give them a piece of my mind when I finally find them. E.R.G.H. This is so unbelievably unprofessional.*

For hours they drilled into me the importance of staying in contact, keeping to the plan and not detouring from it, even the smallest change could completely alter the outcome and put everyone in danger. The only individuals who are in danger now is them, once I get my hands on them, they'll wish they had never lived.

Sparks shoot from my fingertips. I do not notice at first, as my anger continues to boil below the surface of my skin, causing the electrically energised sparks to rapidly multiply. Increasing them in size, next thing I know the street lights around me flutter then completely blackout, leaving me standing in complete darkness in the increasingly humid, sticky street, with an apparently dangerous man. Well, nearly total darkness, sparks still continue to spray haphazardly from my fingertips and now my palms also.

"You should probably learn to control that, before someone who shouldn't sees you like this."

He grabs on to one of my hands, he begins to massage my forearm, before applying what feels like extreme pressure to a specific point on my elbow, disarming the electrical sparks shooting from my hands to stop. I look up to him, surprise smudged over my whole face. I stand there a little longer not sure what to say or do.

"I used to train the students at the school, the one you want the location for. I used to teach them to control and harness their unique abilities. No two were alike, so I had to learn a few tricks of my own, to disable them when things started to get out of control."

He shrugs it off like it was nothing, like taking a breath of air to continue living. I finally manage a nimble reply at best.

"Thank you, I...I suppose I have not had much chance to practice."

I pull my arm back rubbing the area he had applied pressure to. Surprised something so simple could work so effectively.

"If you're wondering, I didn't actually disarm your abilities, I merely distracted you from your emotions. It is a tactic to make the mind focus on something else simultaneously."

He smiles at me, like a father would to his loving child, this man must have loved his students, and I'm sure they loved him. I wonder why they had thrown him out of the school with no recollection of how to find it again? What was it he had done?

But no sooner had he distinguished the sparks from my hands, the hummer miraculously decides to drive around the corner without a care in the world. It pulls up to the curb after seeing me, the window to the back of the stretch hummer goes down. Every movement it does seems to grate on my nerves more and more, every little thing annoys me beyond disbelief.

Sparks fire from my fingertips, a thought comes to me quickly, *Will these sparks burn off my fingerprints?* I shake the idea from my mind, not wanting to distract myself from what was unfolding before me. Small little, short burst of sparks fire from them this time, I try to control it better this time and siphon it in. Not wanting to hurt anyone.

"Hey Tori, you want one?" Logan reaches through the window, with his arm outstretched.

That is the last straw. When Logan shoves a burrito into my face as if we had been here for a night out in the town, stopping for food as if it were the most normal thing in the world.

"So, you're telling me, you left your post, which you made sure to tell me was of the utmost importance, that if I needed you, you would be here for back up. But instead, you went to get Burritos?"

Fumes of smoke feel as though they could be emitting from my body, making me seem to be smoking without actually appearing to be on fire when really, the fire is encased within me, waiting to implode at any given moment.

"I guess we did."

The look in Logan's golden-pooled eyes, shrink into him, as he quickly realises what it is that I am infuriated by, completely lost for words, and not a clue what to say to make it right. He does the one thing he can.

"Chip?"

He raises his other arm from below the window to offer me some of his chips. That's when I lose it, everything around me dims, all I can see now is the flame that burns behind my eyes from my inner core.

I bring my hands up to my waist, clenching them into fists, the sparks now turned into blue flames begin to spread up my arms and then to my body. A surge of energy rushes to my hands, sending a pulse of forcible fire spiralling towards them. The look on Logan's face instantly puts out the flames but it is too late, the hummer has been hit. The flames have been released and are slowly melting the paint off, creating a toxic scent, wafting its smell through the air, one that will haunt my dreams for the rest of my living life.

Next thing I know, when my senses clear and my rage dissipates, the hummer is now on the other side of the street, through a nail salon, with the sign still flashing above the carnage I had just caused. I stare at my arms in shock, what the hell did I just do? Why did I do that? I run over to the hummer to see if Logan is OK. *Please say I haven't killed him, please...*

Chapter 16

Logan is carefully stationed on the side of the road. I have strategically placed myself over his charred body, both my hands placed with my palms over his sternum counting in my head, as I place each compression to his chest, trying to help restart his heat. The guy who had been stood next to me had suggested I use the electrical charge as a jolt, to mimic a defibrillator. But after what had just happened, I do not trust myself to have any kind of handle on my abilities, especially with my emotions so high-strung right now.

"I do not understand, one of the first things they teach at that pretentious school is how to disconnect your emotions from your abilities to stop things like this happening!"

He continues to pace up and down the street, staging the scene as if the services had already arrived. The tape has been placed around the hummer, stopping passersby coming too close. Of course, an actual ambulance has not been called due to the cause of what happened here. It's just me trying to bring back the life I had wrongly taken.

"They clearly have not gotten that far with me yet; can you not tell? Stop shouting unhelpful comments and actually do something helpful, would you."

I scream back at him, wanting his unintentional interrogation to stop.

I look down to see Logan's body still sprawled out underneath me, unmoving, the only rise and fall of his chest comes from me, vigorously trying to bring him back to me.

"Why, why does this keep happening to me?" I land one last extraordinary blow to his chest, giving in to exhaustion. My head now placed onto the top of his lifeless chest. My hand still near his heart that now no longer beats for the life it had once before. Tears begin to pool in the middle of his chest, as I slowly submerge him with the tears that never appear to run out.

I killed him? Am I the monster from the vision I had seen? Am I the one who brings the world around me to its fiery death, leaving nothing behind?

Little sparks flicker from the hand that still wears his heart, with the microscopic amount of energy I have left. My body unexpectedly lets out a few stunted sparks, the first I did not notice but by the third spark, it sends his body arching into a curve, jolting through his back, sending a strong signal to his heart to not give up. I let it continue, scared. Now that I am all too aware it will hurt him further. I try to not interfere with my abilities, letting them do what they feel needs to be done. The sparks progress from my fingers, now situate into the middle of my palm, it sends out one last impulse that sends his body reaching into the air.

Please work, please.

I collapse to the ground next to Logan's unstirring body. Still, I see no sign of life. Too exhausted myself to actually be able to reach over to check his pulse, I lay limply by his side, hoping for a miracle.

I must have passed out from the pure exhaustion, unable to keep myself conscious. I feel a warm hand against my cheek. The sound of a voice that will forever be engraved into my memories, a voice I will never grow tired of hearing. My eyes slowly flutter open to see Logan's face staring down onto my own. The smile on his face is weak but still, he wears it. The look in his eyes is nothing but filled with compassion, where instead should lie hatred and betrayal. I should be the one consoling him, not him, I.

"Logan, I am so sorry; I do not know what came over me. I should not be allowed to use these abilities when all I do is harm those I care most about."

I sit myself up, leaning into his chest, needing to hear it for myself, not believing what I see with my own two eyes.

There in his chest, where it had moments ago laid dormant, now beats a healthy, robust and steady heart. One that I had so wrongly taken away from him, which I could have lost forever. First Ellie, now Logan. Who will be next? Is anyone safe that dares to be within a radius of me? Should I just leave and never come back? At least that way I know those I love will be safe from me.

"Victoria, it is OK, see, I am fine."

Logan raises his arm to his chest then hits it with his fist to signify that he is alive, no thanks to me. I would not have needed to bring him back if it was not from me taking his life in the first place.

"Hey, it was my fault. I should have never given you the impression that I was making you share food with me, of course, I got you your own. Who am I kidding? Of course, I knew you were not going to want to share with me."

Logan tries to laugh in an attempt to lighten the already darkened mood. Trying desperately to stop the tears as they now still fall rapidly down my flushed cheeks. My arms are still tightly wrapped around his waist, never wanting to let go, in fear of losing him again.

"Well, I had, but by the looks of what's left of the hummer, I'm guessing we are going to have to make another trip to the burrito restaurant, that is if you're still hungry, of course."

This time it is me who laughs. I had held it back at first not wanting to give myself the pleasure of feeling happy, not after what I had just done. I am not worthy of ever being allowed to know what that feeling is, after taking two innocent lives from them far too early. But despite what I want, Logan has managed to pry out a laugh from deep within. Only he could be able to do such a thing in a time like this.

"I think you are right. We are going to have to go back, it looks like we may have lost our meals in this tragedy. Sorry." I couldn't help but reply to his playful chatter; after all, he is the one making me laugh after I had just killed him. I slip in another apology, wanting nothing more but for him to know how truly sorry I am for what I had done to him and his friends.

That is when I remember he had not been the only one inside, I quickly stand up to run to the hammer to pry out the remaining bodies from the already dissipated flames.

But it looks like someone has already beaten me to it, I look over to see the group of men who had been inside with him, they seem to be huddled around a body on the floor, I look to see who it may be. The men standing around in an unplanned circle are the tall guy from the plane and Logan's friend. Also, I notice the driver had made it out; that left one unaccounted for, the shorter guy I had yet to get to know. The one that had come up with this whole idea.

I rush over as quickly as I can but not before I double check to make sure Logan is OK. He nods for me to go on without him. Reassuring me that he will be OK for the time being. I place a hand into his, squeezing it in reassurance before hurriedly going over to see what it is that is wrong.

"Is he OK?" As I make my way over the men that had been stood over the body, they shy away, not wanting to get close to me. I suppose I do not blame them after all, I was the one to set them alight.

"He's not breathing," the man from The Bondi Basement is the one to answer my question.

I look to him trying to think of what his name is, did he tell me? Have I just forgotten? Is it rude to now ask for it? Screw it, he has been nothing but helpful the least I can do is remember his name.

"I am so sorry, what is your name? I seem to have forgotten?"

He looks to me unfazed by my question, he clearly has realised I am in dire need of a helping hand, with all things life.

"Jon is my name, Jon Shanks to be exact."

He is unable to read me, which I think unnerves him, making him want to understand what it is I am.

I make my way over to the body, ready to use whatever I have left to help this poor man, after what I had inflicted upon them all, but as I draw closer I notice he is in far worse shape than Logan had been in. His whole is body covered in burns, his clothes in shreds; what's left of them that is. I lean over his bloodied body, the stench of burned flesh strong and stagnant in the humid air that settles around us. I try to hold my breath, not wanting to offend him; the smell is unbearable.

I place both my hands over his chest, starting CPR while trying to force the sparks from my hands, just as I had before. Little at first but slowly they come, I feel my knees begin to heat up as I unintentionally start to draw the energy from the ground beneath me, using it to restart his heart but instead of the sparks I had been able to use on Logan are now no more, as the energy I had drawn from the sun earlier now is replaced with a new energy. One that is useless when it comes to restarting a heart.

Instead of jump starting him back to life, his body begins to break down. What had been his body lying beneath my hands clasped at his chest, trying to get his heart started again, now flakes away in individual dandelion white, delicate puff seeds. The earth taking back the life it had once given, as it is taken back to the earth that had given him the very life I had stolen away from him. I fall down to the ground in a heap of misery, where once his body had been. I scream out in pained frustration, angry for what I had done. I cry, for what it is I have become, feeling more lost and alone than I have ever known to be possible. I stand up in shock, unsure of what it is that is happening. I cry, frustrated with myself, all I want to do is help but all I cause is more pain.

"He was already dead, there was no bringing him back, you did the right honourable thing by giving his soul the release it deserved."

Jon comes over to me, embracing me into a hug as he desperately tries to quiet my shaking body. I am uncontrollably shaking from head to toe, the shock so strong it has left me unable to stand unaided. I killed someone. I am a killer.

Another pair of strong arms are now around me, trying to soothe me but I am not deserving of such actions. They should be pinning me to the ground, stopping me from causing any more harm. My body is beyond shaking now, it is literally vibrating. Both Jon and Logan let go at the exact same time, sending them both in the direction they had come from, taking another deliberate step back each. Oh no, I have captured a new source of power, another one I am unable to control, I do not know how much more of this I can take. After all, I am only one individual who has to channel this potent undiluted energy, healing and reconnecting them. Sending them to where they need to go, each having to go through me first. I will never be able to harness the control. I will need to be who I am destined to be.

Logan takes a hesitant step forward, rightly so. Followed by a hasty jog that leads him right to me.

Quickly wrapping his arms around me, not letting go. Then that is when I feel his thoughts entwining with my own, he's not inside my head like Romeo had been in our dreams but I can feel that he is there. It's his emotions that are now trying to connect to mine, I assume to stabilise them. As it has been made quite visible, I am incapable of doing this alone. He holds on to each one trying to mould it to his own, willing me to let him help. I fight back at first, frightened I will hurt him but he urges me to trust him, to let go and allow him to momentarily take control, to help steer my bubbling emotions in the correct direction, like a sailing ship that had been heading off course about to collide with an oncoming vessel. He continues to soothe me through his own emotions as they slowly begin to mould together, connecting us. Minutes pass, maybe even hours but Logan does not give in. He waits till he can feel every last thread of our emotions tie each and every one to the other, allowing every previous feeling connecting me to my unpredictable power of energies to finally become a stable bomb, no longer ticking over to explode. Eventually, my body dissipates into a normal stance, no longer uncontrollably vibrating from my core.

Logan slowly pulls back but never lets go, to see if I am OK. We both stare longingly into each other's eyes, the connection that has now been evolved between us, now and forever. We can both feel what has now changed between us. Whatever had been there before has multiplied. I can feel it,

Logan can now feel it too. We seem to both automatically know that we have now been connected permanently through our forever entwining emotions. I can feel exactly how he is feeling right now, and he, I. What if he lets go of the hold he has on me right now? Will the connection break? He must have had the same thought as me. Because at that moment, he lets go and purposefully moves his body away from mine.

But to both of our surprise, I can still feel exactly how he feels. The price he now pays for the cost of helping me.

"Let's get going, we need to get on a flight to the Gold Coast before we run out of time," Jon tells us to hurry up, not an ounce of concern or acknowledgment of what had just happened before him.

I look to Logan as he towards me. We both stare confused but knowingly into each other's eyes.

"Let's go. We cannot afford to waste any more time."

He holds out his hand for me to take. I willingly do so, not wanting to feel apart and never alone. Not now that Logan and I are forever connected emotionally.

Chapter 17

I was unable to fall asleep on the plane journey, the unruly chaos running through my turbulent mind. I had actually killed someone. How do I ever get back from that? But to my luck, my emotions do not get the better of me, thanks to Logan now helping me control them. The only thing now is that he can feel everything I feel, and I him. Meaning I know exactly how he feels about me, and he now knows exactly how I feel about his brother? Great! But he can also see how conflicted I am about the two now.

We have decided to book into a hotel for the remainder of the night, well, morning, and try to get as much rest as possible before heading to Jon's friends to find out the location of the school, where evidently Romeo, Logan's brother, is being held.

Logan is passed out next to me on the bed, exhausted from experiencing death then being brought back to life. I suppose that could take a lot out of someone. Leaving them feeling wholly depleted and lifeless. I watch over him. Feeling inordinately protective of him. Ironic really that I should feel this way, considering, I am the one who put his life in danger in the first place. The hotel we have ended up at is nice enough. The view is what gives it that wow factor from the balcony overseeing the ocean. The sky looks as though it could go on forever. I take this time to soak in what is around me, to live solely in this instant. Grounding myself, maybe that might help me manage my obsession.

Ever since hitting the ground at the airport, I have felt every energy as it has absorbed into me to be reconnected to the earth's energy plane; honestly, I forgot that this would be a part of this whole getting used to these abilities. The Elders had told me I am to guide and connect all energies together, keeping the universe balanced. I guess my skills are starting to manifest more, as it seems I have begun absorbing energies without trying. Maybe it is a good thing. Logan and I are now connected emotionally, so I do not explode. Perhaps that's why I can do this now, as my emotions have been stabilised, allowing me to absorb energies around me freely. I still feel a constant light buzz just under the surface of my skin from the power. Every time a new strand of kinetic energy passes through me, I get a jolt of adrenaline filling me with a caffeine shot, energising me. Unfortunately for me, that means I am unable to settle long enough to sleep. I know I should be tired but ever since arriving, I have felt nothing but on edge, in need of a run to release some of this pent-up energy. The pool below is looking like the right choice, one that may help with what I require.

I look through the oversized, reusable shopping bag of clothing I had brought while waiting around for the men to finish eating the whole airport out of food. I had finished mine, surprisingly not feeling overly hungry considering all things, I should be beyond famished but I had barely touched the food sat out in front of me on the table, where all four of us perched ourselves ready to feast.

I decided to go buy myself a change of clothing. My current outfit choice had been slightly more revealing than what I was used to wearing out in public. I also had smelt strongly of smoke. I am also pretty sure I have blood on me still from Logan's wounds. I had picked up a bikini, not actually thinking I would get the time to use it. I thought it would be perfect to wear when we got back but by the looks of it, I might actually get to try out the rich, vibrant red two-piece bathing suit; this specific colour red is stunning against my skin tone. I have been looking for this for so long. Of course, when I finally find it, it would have to be at the airport while on a mission.

Everyone else is asleep. I am quite clearly not going to be joining them, so I might as well make the most of this rare moment of downtime, and clutch on to what I have on offer to me right now. That so happens to be a pool, looking out onto the vast sea that stretches along the strip of beach and buildings. I slide into the soft satin material, enjoying the feel of the smoothness against my skin. It feels incredible, especially after being stuck in leather shorts for hours in this ridiculous humidity.

I quickly pop into the bathroom and grab a complimentary towel. Just as I open the door to leave, I realise how exposed I felt, and had continued to feel over the last stretched out hours. So, I decide to run back in and chuck on the oversized t-shirt I had bought as well. Glad that I had chosen to go for comfort and practicality when buying the clothing.

I make my way down the stairs, taking every chance I have to release this feeling, opting out of the lift, which is the obvious, lazier option for myself. I look through the halved window door and around getting a better idea of the layout. Once through the door leading to the pool, I notice a steam room. I'll have a go at that later.

I hear a knock at the door, so I put the towel in my hand onto the lounger by the pool and walk over to see who it could be? Maybe someone forgot their access card? As I steadily make my way over to the door, while also trying not to slip over on the glistening wet marble floor, I move carefully, distracted suddenly by a splash made in the pool. Is there someone else in here with me? I am sure I did not see anyone else... I am going to turn my head back to prove to myself that I could not have possibly missed someone else being present. The individual at the door continues pushing and pulling, trying to get it to unhinge itself. I mutter under my breath for this impatient person to calm down, I am on my way. I cannot go any faster without risking humiliating myself in front of this stranger. I have had enough of that recently.

"Alright, keep your trousers on, I'm coming."

The words fall from my mouth impatiently.

Abruptly, and ruthlessly, I am swept off my feet and into the air. The next thing, before I have the chance to fight back, everything goes unseeingly black after a sharp deliberate blow to the back of my head, followed by a short blood-curdling scream as I feel myself being submerged under water. My cries becoming increasingly muffled by the water as it quickly and rapidly closes in on me. The further I am ruthlessly dragged deeper, more buried under the surface of the water, breaking every layer as I am unfairly pulled to the depths of my deep unconscious mind, leaving me defenceless. Everything happens too quickly for me to be able to register and react swiftly, showing precisely how untrained I frightfully am, before surrendering to the darkness.

Flashes of light break through sporadically, as I gain consciousness momentarily throughout the journey. The first time I start to come to, one of the nearby voices begins to panic, hitting me with a hard-edged object, sending me spiralling back into the deepest depths of the dreadfully dark part of my unconscious mind, leaving me vulnerable, and susceptible to incoming, and highly unwanted visions from the Elders.

Flickers of images barrel their way through my darkened mind, leaving spots of light. Every time one makes its way through, a spinning wheel of images play out behind my heavy closed eyelids, leaving their imprints behind forever, never being able to unsee what I have now been shown.

The image starts with me standing in a field, one that has been scorched from the sun beating down upon it relentlessly, not given an inch, leaving the crops and fields around each other parched, and tirelessly searching for water to quench its dying thirst. I look around myself, trying to find any sign of life other than my own. My hands are transfixed to either side of me, unable to move.

The energy from the earth below me pulls me to its need, to connect it back to the elements around it. Someone or something has willingly unhinged the links to which the earth is generated through, leaving it deranged and unable to reconnect itself. To be able to rebuild itself through the energy that is water is now lost, flowing around without direction or purpose, its energy life source is broken and lost in the vast open space, leaving it in a state of evaporation, unable to do what it is intended for. Fuelling and hydrating the life around it, or what's left of it. I know without having to be told that I am the one, and the only one who can fix this mess. The climate around me is heating above the temperature that is required to sustain life itself. The polar ice caps melting at a substantial rate. If I do not recreate the balance that is needed, life will cease to exist as we know it.

I lethargically try opening my eyes but close them shut quicker than I could open them, as the light shining pains them. Reminding me of the multiple blows to the head momentarily as my head pounds against my skull, throbbing uncontrollably without any sign of immediate surrender. *What the hell happened to me? Better yet, who did this to me? Ouch. Maybe this is a result of the blunt force trauma to my head, mixed with the unwarranted vision of the world coming to an end, I undoubtedly will be left to fix on my own.* I go to move my arm, to touch the back of my head but find that I am unable to, due to my arms being suspended above my head, shackled by some sort of binding tethered to my wrists.

Oh my goddess! How am I meant to draw the energy from around me if I am unable to access my hands? I really need to learn how to kick my senses into autopilot at will. *Where am I?* Tears start to full down my face, streaming through the cracks on my skin, stinging as it passes over cuts and bruises. What the...? I feel as though I have lost a fight that I do not remember partaking in. I try to reach my fingers to my wrists on my other arm. Can I figure it out? I fidget and squirm endlessly but nothing gives way. After what feels like hours or even days, I hear a faint voice in the distance, talking to someone, followed by footsteps. As the footsteps get closer, the voices grow louder. What I had thought was one before, turn out to be many.

I scream for help hoping they hear me, hoping they are here to help me. I scream again for the help. The agony that penetrates through my bloodied body drenches my words for help. *Please, someone, help me!* I cry, still. It is pointless, the words do not pass my lips, for they stay trapped inside my head. Screaming for help to no one but myself. I feel stiff, stuck like in quicksand. My body feels foreign, like it no longer belongs to me. I command it to move, for my voice to be heard but the more I struggle, the harder it gets. It is as though my body is fighting against me, no longer wanting to be a part of me. I try to scream again but this time, my throat slowly closes in on itself. I struggle to breathe. I gasp for air but it is coming far less now. I'm entirely motionless, unable to move, talk and now breathe. Inside my head, I am crashing side to side, grasping for my throat to open its airways again. To allow the air, I need to flow through and sustain the oxygen my body needs. When it feels like there is no hope, a singular voice speaks to me, one that I have not heard before.

"Quit fighting it, the more you struggle, the faster it will kill you. It is like you have never witnessed enchantment energy before. If you struggle, it will only tighten its grip on you, starting with each of your ligaments, then slowly starts to shut down all your organs until you are left with one last breath."

I go to scream one last time but it is pointless. My eyes flash open in one last hope, to somehow tell the person before me to help. I suck in my last dying breath before slowly feeling my body fall away from me, feeling less and less, until I feel as light as a feather, floating away in the wind. Finally, at peace.

I am woken suddenly, to the sound of an angry, disgruntled voice.

"Did you not hear me when I said it is best to stop struggling? It only gets worse."

The unnamed person begins to untie me. I appear to be laying on a solid floor, grateful not to be suspended above the ground, hanging from my weak wrists and arms, the wall I had clung to no longer holds me hostage. I suck in a rare rush of light-filled oxygen. Air has never tasted and felt so good. Apart from the raw, dry and scratchy feeling in my throat, I feel OK.

My thoughts are interrupted by the voice chanting.

"Undo what has been, for what it is, does not belong upon an innocent. Evacuate from an unearthed child, undo what has been wrongly done."

A wave of warmth rushes over my entire body, as though kissed by sunlight. I welcome the feeling. I embrace it. Never have I ever been so grateful for the pure blissfulness to wash over me after such a shitty day.

I place my hands on either side of me to hold myself up, my body begins to automatically absorb the energy radiating from the ground beneath me. I move my neck from side to side, cracking the stiffness away. Why hadn't my body just taken over before, getting me out of this situation before it got this far?

The person that had helped me now stands to stare at me while the complete absorption of energy takes place.

"You're one of them, aren't you?"

They continue to watch, every detail is carefully registered and stored away to memory, clear interest adamant across their face.

"One of them?" the words scratch their way up my throat in reply to my saviour.

Chapter 18

Mismatched slabs of various paving stones clutter their way through the room. I scan through the place to catalogue every little detail throughout, to put it away for later use, knowing I will have to come back here once I figure a way out. Why would anyone want to kidnap me? Your guess is as good as mine.

"You are one of those kids from that fancy, super private school, that is if your family is not well known or super stinking rich, you get left out to defend for yourself. While within those walls, you get full training and accommodation." The underlying tone of their voice suggests they are aggravated by this fact. It has clearly been thought about a lot, grating and pulling at their nerves, slowly growing and festering beneath the surface, for what seems to be an extended period.

"I do not know what you're talking about."

I try to betray my innocence on the whole matter when, in reality, I have a fair idea of what they are referring to.

I could have sworn there was more than one person on their way into me. I had heard the voices to go along with the multiple footsteps. I look to the one that had made their way through, to subsequently save me. But if this person was the one to take me in the first place, why help me now?

"Where are the others? The ones who had been with you just before?"

I look up to see the eyes that had been drenched in kindness on helping me, now liquefied by hatred and frustration. I need to find out about everyone that is here or near, so I can plan accordingly to get out of this damp, wet and unhygienic excuse of a hideout. If I play my cards right, who knows I might actually help myself out for once.

"Others?"

A line forms between the individual's brows as they allow what I had just said to sort its way through the mind that had otherwise been occupied on something far away from here.

"Yes," I confirm, knowing that the question had been rhetorical but I answer anyway. In hopes of urging a reply.

"There are no others, only I. You see, my ability is a rare one, one that allows me to multiply myself limitlessly without ever exceeding anything anyone could possibly imagine. What you had mistaken for others was in reality only I."

The individual stands up straighter then, pride clear across their face, what had been bothering them before now clearly forgotten, for now that is.

OK, this can either work out to my advantage or could go horribly wrong, who knows? But I am about to find out.

I focus my thoughts on pushing the energy out of me, to the person in front. Willing them to be gone but instead to my dismay, flowers upon flowers shoot from my now outstretched hand, leaving the person amused, if that, and now a glorified flower maid. *What the—?* I look to my hands, confused really, why on earth are there flowers? Last I checked, I am in a hole in the middle of nowhere surrounded by dirt.

"Interesting, I could have sworn you had the ability to manipulate fire."

One of the flowers that lay at their feet is now held steadily in my previously thought saviour's hand which currently is being made apparent they are anything but. Are they my captor? Unquestionably if they had come to save me, we would have left this God-awful place by now.

"That's a pity, the last flower girl I had brought down here lay exactly where you now sit. The only difference is, I cut her throat and watched her bleed out slowly before my very own eyes, her hand had been clutched up to her throat, in an attempt to stop the bleeding that had led to her timely death."

They continue to twirl the eloquently beautiful petaled flower in between their fingers, never once breaking eye contact with me. Lifting their own arm up to rest their hand on their neck to adequately portray what had happened precisely where I am now placed.

I guess that answers that question. I need to get out of here now!

"You see, I have no need for that gift. If I had, I would have kept the last pretty little thing instead of killing her." The eyes that had been transfixed onto my very own now shift suddenly to an object I had not known was there before, it now glistens in the dim light, showing me its sharp teeth ready to doom me to the same terrible fate of those that had come before me.

"It is a shame that you do not possess the ability I need, I could have sworn I saw you hold, and wield the fire to your need. Oh well, I have no need for you."

They slowly walk over to the unlit corner of the room to where the axe now appears to have its own stage light, showing exactly how frightened I should be. It lays up against the far wall. I need to do something. I need to move away from this spot. I have absorbed the girl that had died here before me. I have incorporated her ability within me, diluting the energy of the sun I had held. I can feel her gurgled screams as her life slithered relentlessly away from her.

I stand up abruptly, and make a beeline for the door. As I do, I hear footsteps coming up fast behind me, just inside of the doorway lays a mirror, a strange place to be had but it will have to do. I place my hand onto the mirror, quickly adding its energy to my power bank. Before I have a chance to fully load, the back of my legs buckle beneath me, from the might of the axe, as it forces itself upon me.

Now leaving my knees fixed to the ground, not entirely cutting through like I am sure they had hoped but the gash left behind agonises me. I spin my head around to see where I can aim my rage, channelling it through my arms, centring it through the palm of my hand at my once thought saviour. Shards of glass come soaring now, hitting the centre of their broad chest. The body falls back, and into the spot they had evidently taken an innocent life. The glass that had missed falls to the ground but as it does it opens up. I hear laughter echoing its way through, what was that? Before I can go over and expect it, it vanishes away. I look back to the mirror and focus everything I have onto it. Keeping my eyes away from the pool of blood that now soaks the ground.

The mirror opens itself up to me, swirls of purple and silver mixing together like a bowl of paint. A feeling takes over, and I know what to do. I focus on where I need to be, better yet where I want to be.

A picture surfaces in front of me, a bright hall full of colour, young adults walking up and down the hall. Could it be? Is this the school we have all been looking for? Right here at my fingertips.

I wonder what would happen if I push my hand against the rippling image. Not expecting it to give way like a pastry base as it crumbles in your hands. I allow my body to fall into it, not able to stand up from the trauma inflicted to my legs. As I begin to fall, I take one last look back, and there, walking up the stairs I had used to get away, is the same individual with an axe in hand I could have sworn I saw sprawled out over the mismatched flooring with their blood spilled chaotically around them, but now I see the dark depths of the hatred held within their eyes. I look away, putting my full weight into the mirror now, wanting to get away as fast as possible.

Just as my legs go to follow the rest of me, a piercing, loud snap, followed by an otherworldly pain shoots its way through me. Now I just fall, fall to the depths of the void within the mirror, hoping that I will not be lost forever and make it to where I want to be.

My head spins uncontrollably as I descend through the voids that lead the way before me, I come tumbling down in a heap of filth and blood, straight onto clean, fresh carpets, the same ones that had lined the halls of the school I had seen before me in the image of the mirror.

"Crap!"

I pull myself onto my back to inspect the damage that had been inflicted to my lower legs. One of them appears to be hanging by shreds of muscle, tendons, and skin from what I can see from the front and the back. Well, the axe didn't miss its intended use the second or possibly even the first time. It has cut through all the fat, skin, muscle and bone from severing its way through the back, not stopping before it completely cut through, leaving me without a foot from just above the ankle, or where it used to be. The midsection of my calf is left bloodied and carved from the first inflicted blow. Blood is pulsating, leaving the clean, vibrant carpet around me drenched in my own blood.

This is not good at all. I need to get outside to where the grass is grown from the pure Mother Earth, to rebuild and repair the damage that has been done. I look around me to see if there is anyone around who could help me, or if there is no one, a door that leads me to outside. One that takes me to a field would be highly preferred.

I try soaking the energy from around me to see if it can help at all. Forgetting momentarily that I am sat directly in my own puddle of blood.

The blood platelets surrounding me begin to rise and gather around me, filtering through a pure white light, then descending down to be reabsorbed by my body, going back to where it had come from once before. The dizzy feeling and light-headedness I had been feeling begins to dissipate, leaving my thought process easy to file through.

I may not have completely fixed the problem but at least it's something. I feel like I should be able to pull myself to an exit somewhere. First, I take the baggy top off that I had chucked on last minute, thankfully, and rip along the bottom seem. After I get the piece of material I need, I chuck it back on, not wanting to be left crawling along the floor in my vibrant red bikini I had put on earlier that day.

Leaving me with a long thick lengthened piece of material, enough to be able to tie around my lower leg to keep it in place for as long as possible, while I find a way to repair it.

Knowing far too well that my foot had stayed behind, not coming through the mirrored portal with the rest of me. For now, I can only apply pressure to minimise the blood loss. I work quickly, wanting to reattach the blood flow to the semi-detached leg part, consisting of my calf on my other leg, the one that still possesses a foot. Knowing full well that if it does not get done soon, I will lose it for good. I may be able to heal but replacing limbs might be a tad far-fetched. After fastening the makeshift bandage to the wounded area, I adjust the now shortened shirt I had been wearing. Not wanting to be seen army crawling my way through the school's halls in just a red bikini and one semi-detached leg and one fully detached foot. Not the best first impression if I might say so myself.

I slowly start to pull myself along the floor, as slowly but as fast as my body will allow. The pain to the remaining leg that has lost a foot is unbearable but to my luck, the one that is barely holding on is painless, which is not a good sign. I vaguely start taking in my surroundings trying to use it as a distraction while also looking for a door that looks like it would lead to outside. The school seems similar to the tunnels I had been to under my school back in New Zealand. Very clean, carpeted floor, modernised look to it. I push a few doors open, which only lead to empty classrooms or empty halls, a few of them do not move at all from being locked. I can feel my body weakening again from losing the blood I had reabsorbed. I do not know how much longer I can go on for. How on earth is it possible that I have not come across a single person in this massive school? Am I even in the right place? Maybe I am back at the tunnels in New Zealand. It does look the same but different too, but that might just be from the blood loss.

My eyes grow more burdensome, and my pace slows down drastically. I am fading fast. I am running out of options quickly. I try one last door, hoping it will be the one. I push it with everything I have left.

But to my dismay, I am welcomed by another empty room, full of computers, rows, and rows with yet no one using them. How can this be?

Do these people not go outside to breathe? Are there no emergency exits? But just as that last thought echoes through my mind, the vast emptiness I have been continuously greeted with over and over again has now taken over my mind, leaving me in utter darkness once again.

Leaving me in a void of nothing.

The glow from the bright light is ever growing, not stopping to worry about those around it, blinding anyone who dares to look upon it with their naked eyes. As groggy as I am, the light does nothing to help me. I mutter under my breath for someone to turn it off.

"Can you turn that thing off?"

I get no response, which does not surprise me but then I feel a pressure against my leg, astonished by the feeling I am met with. I open my eyes, not caring now that the blinding light is obviously uncomfortable. But once my eyes flutter open, I realise the light is coming from me, the same light I had seen when healing Ellie back at the forest. I am also met with the same eyes that had helped me save her life.

I look down to my leg, the worst image comes to play in my mind, I was too late. I look down, and all I see is a stump to were my foot had once before been held in place by the connection of my ankle, which I had thought had also been lost forever but it seems to have healed and regrown, but failing to complete the full reconstruction. I bury my head deep into the cold, damp ground, which to my relief is covered in grass and soil. I take both hands and place them to my sides, drawing all the energy I can from around me to heal what I had lost.

When I am physically unable to hold anymore within me, I let it flow through me and centre it towards where my foot had been. Imagining what it had looked like, to will it to grow again, like it had once before when I had been created within my mother's womb.

"You won't be able to, you still need to fully heal and recharge before you can try anything like that."

I hear the voice but I carry on anyway.

"It was too late, it had already died off, I am sorry but you cannot get it back."

The voice of the boy who is my familiar tries to bring me comfort in this time but all I do at that moment is roll over into the earth beneath me and cry.

Cry for the foot I had taken for granted and would do anything to get back.

What good are these abilities if I cannot do this one simple thing?

The tears are endless, streaming down my blood smeared face. The events that have led up to this moment, show through my mind, making me twist up into myself.

I will kill whoever it was that did this to me!

My familiar who had yet again saved me, leans down to soothe me with a deliberate but calming pat on the back.

"I made you this, it should help you get around. I know it is not the real thing. But it will help."

I look to my familiar then as he hands me over a prosthetic foot, to attach to my stump.

I purposefully wipe away my tears. *Get up, Victoria, you cannot afford to lay here and feel sorry for yourself.* I take it from him.

"Thank you."

I sob, less now. As I try to gather myself, I lean over and examine it for a while, then I decide when I have had enough time to wallow and quickly put it on.

It feels strange, heavy, unnatural. But I stand up anyway to get used to it, and to see if it will allow me to walk.

It does…

I should be grateful I am alive, for so many have had their lives taken far too soon.

I look to my familiar who looks to me, then to a door that leads back inside.

I think he wants me to follow him, so I do. Maybe he knows where to find Romeo. After everything that has happened, finding Romeo seems like a distant memory from the person I had started out as.

One can only hope.

I walk till I reach the halls I had relentlessly dragged myself along to get outside, now I am willingly walking back. Well, hobbling, I am still getting used to this new foot of mine.

The silhouette of a young girl materialises before me, it unsuspectedly comes to my attention that for some unknown entity, I am unable to pull my reluctant gaze away. I have this constant growing feeling I know this girl. She is yet to entirely turn around so I can identify her. Who could she be? Why do I feel this lingering connection to this individual, when I have yet to see her face? This masked stranger does not feel like a stranger to me at all. She stands with a group of other fellow students who attend this expansive and extraordinary school, based strategically in Australia for those with unique abilities.

I am overly eager for the unknown individual to turn around, to see why I am so undeniably drawn to them. I can feel her energy force looming near me, wanting to connect us indifferently. Why is this? Should I allow it? I have not felt any form of energy force like this before, yet it feels familiar to me, like a second skin. Connecting to it would be effortless. I decide to side on the chance of caution, instead of connecting with it unknowingly. Without fully understanding what is happening, I roll in the energy instead, pulling it towards me, without ever letting it get close enough, to fully emerge in the connection effortlessly forming before us.

The reason I am toying with this energy force, not allowing it to connect with me and all other energies, is that it feels kind of final, like it will bring it to an end. I do not know how else to explain it. But I am hoping that with me pulling it close and letting it go again, will get the attention of the young individual, resulting in her alternatively turning around, so I can finally make sense of all these crazy feelings, rushing around frantically inside of my very being. Sparks are quite literally flying off of me.

My energy force seems to be almost malfunctioning. Is this is even possible? I try one more time to pull it towards me, holding it longer this time. I begin to feel critically fatigued the longer I pursue this tactic but I am unwilling to give in yet, a little longer will not hurt anyone I hope? Maybe me.

Just when I am about to give up on my unreserved efforts, pathetically giving up on my pesky attempt to get her attention, most reasonable people would just go up to the individual, and simply say "Hello."

Apparently, I am no longer normal.

The girl swirls around swiftly with minimal effort required, the look of utter shock and recognition evident on her face. She must have felt when I reluctantly let go of her energy source, it sprang back quicker than an elastic band, probably resembling the same sharp pain, inflicting what it would have felt like as if it had actually hit her bare skin.

I summon up what I have left of my ever-draining energy, regretting holding on so long. I feel completely depleted, I need to borrow some energy from the entities around me, so I can function effectively. I look up to see the girl staring right at me, the look on her face now mirrored onto my own. She speaks before I have the chance to, too shocked to be able to form an articulated, audible and coherent sentence.

"Victoria?"

All she had to say was that one word, to send shivers catapulting down my spine, the look of pure disbelief. Adamant and fixated on her beautifully familiar face. I would recognise those delicately structured features encased inside of that vibrant red hair, perfectly resembling my mother's. Ours.

"Rose?" I finally manage to string together an intelligible, clear, lucid sound, letting it rip its way through my tiresome mouth.

How could this be? She is meant to be lying in a hospital bed in one of London's best-facilitated hospitals, fighting for her life in a coma?

A single tear falls rapidly down my flushed pink cheek. She runs toward me, and I to her. One word escaping my bewildered lips.

"Rose."